This edition published in the UK in 2024

Copyright © Michael Fardon 2024

The right of Michael Fardon to be identified as the author of this work has been asserted under the Copyright, Designs and Patents Act 1988.

All rights reserved. No part of this publication may be reproduced, stored in a retrieval system, or transmitted in any form or by any means, electronic, mechanical, photocopying, recording or otherwise, without the prior written consent of the publishers.
All characters and incidents in this publication are fictitious. Any resemblance to real persons living or dead, events or localities is purely coincidental.

Text and cover design by Caroline Goldsmith.
Cover image: iStock Photo

Also available as an ebook edition

Through
Dark Waters

Michael Fardon

This book is dedicated to my wife, Anne, and our daughter, Sarah, without whose great enthusiasm, proofreading and other advice this book would not have been possible.

Chapter 1

The last dance at the university leavers' ball was about to take place for final-year students. But not for Dan – dark-haired, bearded, shy and lanky – who was propping himself up at the students' union bar, watching the dancing. He was very much on his own, gripping an empty pint glass and sadly watching his fellow students getting ready for the final dance.

But there was no dance partner for Dan. It really was the end for him. He had only, in the previous week, been suddenly dumped by his very attractive and much-loved girlfriend, Helen. Out of the blue she had broken up their two-year very close relationship. Their final encounter had ended badly, with an argument and shouting and tears. Helen told Dan that he was 'just not right' for her any more. And that became the end of their story.

And so he now watched from the bar as his fellow final-year students gathered together with their partners for the last dance. What Dan really wanted was to find a new partner for this dance to show

Helen that he did not need her any more. He put down his empty glass and made his way over to the dance floor. The lights dimmed and the music started to work its soft erotic magic. The couples began moving closer and closer to each other.

Then the unexpected happened. Dan caught sight of a girl he had very much fancied and had a fling with in his first year at uni. Her name was Amy, a shapely, sensual and red-headed Irish girl with a reputation. Everybody knew about 'hot Amy.' She was known for her promiscuity and openness about sex. And Dan had already experienced a boozy night with her and a 'back to my room' steamy session. In fact he had later dated her on a number of occasions and had taken quite a shine to her. But then, in his second year, he had met Helen who had changed everything.

And now Dan could see Amy on the edge of the dance floor, all alone and staring and smiling at him suggestively. Then she was waving him over, her inviting eyes fixed on him, her flame-red hair curling over a revealing black dress. It was now his turn to smile. She blew him a kiss and stretched out her hands as he approached. He was drawn by her into the middle of the dance floor, and then her arms were around him, pulling him closer and tighter.

When the band had finished, there was a pause as the couples stood still, close together and swaying before moving to the bar or setting off into the night. Amy stared into Dan's eyes and whispered in a low voice, pulling him closer and closer.

'Hmm, and so you're mine again, Dan. I so much love that.'

'And so do I,' replied Dan, who was getting hungry

for her. Amy pulled him away from the other dancers towards the exit.

'Let's go back to my room,' she whispered, 'I need you, my man.'

Amy's hall of residence was a ten minute walk away on the campus, but for Dan and Amy it took longer as they stopped in dark corners, holding each other close, kissing and fondling. Eventually they reached Amy's room and after frantic unzipping and unbuttoning, Amy pushed Dan down on her bed. She knew what she wanted from him and he knew too. He was entering paradise. When it was all over they lay back on the bed, gasping, and then fell into a long deep sleep.

****

Dan woke up next morning, thinking that he must have been dreaming. But no, it was all very real. Amy was there next to him, fast asleep, snoring gently, her hair in a red tangle. When she eventually woke up they did not leave the bed for some time, instead lying together and cuddling. But time marched on and Amy reluctantly released herself and got out of bed, leaving Dan where he was. He watched every movement she made with her body as she put on a dressing gown and then slowly brushed her long, flame-red hair. But Dan was suddenly woken from his dreamy thoughts when Amy turned around in alarm and held out her watch.

'Oh my God, Dan, look at the time. My parents will be arriving to pick me up very soon. I really don't want them to find us like this.'

'Oh shit,' muttered Dan as he got up and started to pull on his clothes, which were scattered across the floor.

'We will see each other again, won't we?' Amy asked as she frantically got all her belongings together.

'Don't you worry,' he replied. 'We certainly will.'

'So don't bloody forget me,' she exclaimed.

'No way,' replied Dan.

They hastily exchanged telephone numbers. Dan pulled her close to him, gave her a final kiss and rapidly disappeared down the stairs, leaving her to get ready for her parents' arrival and the journey back home.

Dan now had a long wait, back in his own uni room, surrounded by suitcases and other belongings. He looked at his watch. His parents were due to pick him up at lunchtime and take him to Birch Cottage, their summer retreat in a town called Leigh Witcombe in the rural Cotswolds. He wandered down to the refectory and grabbed a quick breakfast, wondering what lay in store for him and Amy after such a night spent together. Life had certainly taken a turn for the better. It had been something special. They would definitely need to meet up somehow or other. And soon.

A couple of hours later, Dan's parents, Ollie and Maggie, were knocking at his door and bringing him back to reality. He opened it and Maggie enveloped him in a big hug. Ollie, meanwhile, was staring at what had to go in the car. He groaned at the sight of boxes of books and papers, suitcases, pictures, and bags full of shoes.

'Well,' exclaimed Ollie, grinning at Dan, 'This will be the last time we will be doing this trip, won't it?

At least I hope so, given all this stuff of yours.'

'I guess so,' muttered a grumpy Dan under his breath as they started to load up the car. Ollie was always making a joke of Dan.

After five or so minutes of heaving and puffing, the job was done and the Barnes' car was heading to Birch Cottage. The cottage was one of several properties that Dan's father owned. It was a journey filled with chat as they caught up on news.

'Well, Dan, we have some news for you. Matt is staying at the cottage this weekend.' Matt was his twin brother. The two had been very close during their childhood. There had been one incident where Dan had been off sick with a bad cold and so was at home with his mother whilst his brother was at the school they both attended. Little Dan had insisted that they drive to school because Matt 'was hurt'. His mother had been baffled and convinced Dan must be running a fever. That was, until she had a call from the school informing her that Matt had taken a severe injury in a rugby match. Somehow his brother had felt the pain of the head injury that had caused him a major concussion.

Matt hadn't gone to university, choosing instead to go straight out and work. The brothers were close, though, and spoke on the phone every week. Matt had clearly decided to surprise his brother upon his return home.

'Oh great,' replied Dan.

'He has brought that new girlfriend, Lisa, with him. She's a charming girl.'

Matt had told Dan about Lisa. They had met at a bar and Dan knew his brother was quite smitten.

'Great news,' exclaimed Dan. 'I can't wait to see him. And meet Lisa, of course.'

He decided to say nothing to his parents at this stage about what had happened with Helen or Amy. They chatted for a while about university events, and then Dan fell asleep on the rear seat. The previous night had been fun but also long and exhausting.

Eventually the car arrived at Birch Cottage. Home at last. Dan and his parents were welcomed by Matt and Lisa with hugs, smiles and a cooked supper. Lisa was a stunningly beautiful and slim blonde. Soon after the meal, Ollie and Maggie went to bed, leaving Dan, Matt and Lisa to drink whisky and catch up with family news.

'You are a dark horse,' exclaimed Dan to Matt, tongue in cheek. 'How on earth did you manage to convince this lovely lady to go out with you. I am very envious.' Dan grinned across the table at Lisa. She smiled back at him.

'So how did you two meet?' asked Dan.

'You tell him, Matt,' said Lisa, putting her hand on his arm.

'OK. So we were both at the same bar in Bristol. I saw her. Couldn't help but ask for her number. And – to my surprise – she gave it to me.'

'And we haven't looked back since,' Lisa laughed.

'So, Dan,' said Matt, changing the subject, 'how are things with you? I'm so sorry that things with Helen didn't work out.'

Dan suddenly looked serious. He cleared his throat before he replied.

'Yes. Me too. I'm doing OK.'

'She was a clever girl. And a real looker,' Matt said.

'But,' Dan paused, 'I am now seeing another girl. And I hope you will meet her soon. Her name is Amy and she is Irish.'

'You don't hang about, do you?' exclaimed Matt. 'So, when did this happen?'

'Well, it did all happen rather quickly.'

'Bloody hell!' Matt exclaimed. 'So when are we going to meet her? Why didn't you invite her this weekend?'

'Well, it's all a bit new. If you must know, it all happened last night, at the end of the college year, during the last dance in fact.'

'Wow. Well, I'm happy for you, bro.'

The brothers then carried on chatting, exchanging news and laughing at jokes. But Lisa began to yawn and lean close to Matt.

'Time for bed, I think,' she said softly to him. 'I really need some shuteye.'

The love birds got up to go, leaving Dan to make his own way up to his old bedroom to sleep and to dream of Amy.

****

The following morning Matt and Lisa drove off, leaving Dan to catch up with his parents in the cottage. In the evening Dan received a text message from Matt:

> 'Dan, it was great seeing you. Lisa thinks you are really lovely, so you have certainly scored there. I hope all goes well with your new girl.'

Dan texted back:

> 'Thanks Matt. It was good to meet Lisa. You are a lucky man.'

And so Dan was left with his parents in the family cottage thinking about Amy but he couldn't help but also think about Lisa who he had secretly and enviously thought very attractive.

Chapter 2

Dan and Amy were getting closer and closer. As the summer weeks passed by, their relationship developed and deepened. Dan based himself at Birch Cottage to be closer to Amy's hometown. They got temporary jobs enabling them to afford to spend weekends together on the creaking beds of B&Bs in Woodham, a country town conveniently situated halfway between their homes. Their relationship was a passionate one. The hot magic of the last dance had not been forgotten.

The lovebirds were in regular contact until one Monday when Amy failed to return Dan's phone calls and messages. Silence. Tuesday and Wednesday passed by. Still no contact. Dan wondered what had happened.

On Thursday, in the late evening, Amy called him, but he missed the call because he was out with some mates. She had left a voice message which he picked up as he got back home. Her voice was quiet and subdued. Not at all like her normal chirpy and cheerful self.

'Hi, Dan. Please call me. This is something urgent. Love you.'

Dan was worried. What the hell was going on? Was she going to give him the push as well? He had experienced enough heartbreak with Helen. It was late but he phoned Amy. When she picked up she still sounded quiet and reserved. Definitely not the normal Amy.

'Dan, I need to talk to you about something important, but I can't tell you over the phone. We really need to meet up.'

'I don't get this, Amy. Why can't we talk now? I have been worried sick about you. Where the hell have you been? You haven't been returning any of my messages.'

'Dan, I really do need to see you. This weekend. In Woodham? Can you come?'

Dan paused trying to collect his thoughts together.

'OK then, Amy,' he eventually replied. 'Usual place and time, in Woodham this Saturday. I'll book us a room.'

'Thanks Dan— Oh no... sorry, the front door bell is ringing. Shit! Must go.'

Amy rapidly cut off the call. Dan decided to go to bed, but sleep for him was intermittent. What was Amy's problem? Was she going to dump him? If so, what was it about his girlfriends? Or what was it about him?

Saturday arrived. Dan and Amy met and decided to go for their usual walk in the park near to Woodham Church. The church clock was chiming twelve and the sunshine meant the day was baking hot. Amy took his arm, and they walked to a secluded and shady corner of the park. Dan looked quizzically at her as they sat down on a bench. Amy turned to him, awkwardly taking his hands in hers.

'I'm pregnant, Dan.' She said it quickly.

Dan said nothing. He stared at her, not knowing what to think or what to say. Amy looked desperate.

'For fuck's sake, please say something, Dan.'

Dan took a breath and then spoke quietly and slowly.

'I am sorry, Amy. I don't know what to say. I really can't take all this in. It has come as such a shock. We've always used protection. How did this happen?'

'I don't know. I guess they say that no protection is a hundred percent effective. I didn't believe it either and so I took a second pregnancy test and it was positive.'

Dan fell silent again. Amy was becoming exasperated. The park had suddenly become quiet and it seemed to Dan that even the birds were no longer singing. After a long pause he looked up at Amy.

'So, what do we do now? I mean, what options do we have?' he asked.

'What do you mean?' Amy looked shocked. 'You weren't thinking of…? Oh no! No way! You can't be suggesting I get rid of it. Dan, abortion is out of the question. I really do want to keep this baby. It's *our* baby. And I can't imagine what my parents would do if I told them I was getting an abortion.'

Dan was lost for words.

Amy continued, still grasping his hands in hers. 'Dan, think about it – *our* baby. This will be our love child. I think this is meant to be. Maybe you and I are meant to be, too?' Amy's eyes were welling up with tears. Pleading.

Dan put his arm around Amy and held her tight. She was shaking and sobbing. He cleared his throat and answered her in a quiet serious voice.

'Yes, I am with you on this. This is our baby. It will be an adventure for us and we can build a family. And I promise I will work my socks off to support us.'

'Thanks, Dan,' Amy replied. 'I love you so much.' She paused for a moment. 'If it's a girl I want to call her Maya. I love that name. It means dream and love.'

'A good choice,' said Dan. 'Maya sounds right. It's a lovely name.'

'If it's a boy... well, I don't really know.'

'How about Oliver?' suggested Dan. 'My father's name – except that he is called Ollie by nearly everyone. What do you think?'

'Hmmm,' said Amy. 'Maybe not Oliver. It sounds old-fashioned to me. Mind you, I am sure my parents will suggest Irish names. I suppose I will have to tell them now.'

They remained on the seat in the park for a while, the two of them. They said nothing, both of them contemplating and listening to the sound of children playing in a nearby playground. As the church clock chimed the quarter hour they set off to their B&B, hand-in-hand. They felt that they had something to celebrate now. They were excited. And they were also scared.

Seven months later

Amy was now full-term, and very early one Friday morning her waters broke. Amy's parents had been shocked at the news that she was pregnant and insisted that she and Dan get married immediately. Dan and Amy had gently refused but told them that they would be living together and could be a family. Ollie and Maggie were far more practical and offered Dan and Amy Birch Cottage to live in until they got on their feet. Dan got a good job as a salesman for Leichmatic, a kitchen design company with headquarters based in Germany. He sometimes thought he could have done better with his degree qualification but the salary was solid and he had a baby to think about now.

That Friday morning, Dan was released by his boss and rushed Amy by car to the nearby Milchester City Hospital. Within hours, she had given birth to a healthy, seven-pound baby girl. Her name, as planned, was Maya Elizabeth. Amy was exhausted but ecstatically happy, lying on the bed in the delivery room, talking to Dan, with the baby by her side.

'Come on now,' exclaimed Amy. 'It's your turn to hold your daughter.' She looked up at Dan, beaming. 'She looks so much like you with those brown eyes and dark hair.'

Dan took the little bundle in his arms, looked down at his daughter and welled up. Maya Elizabeth was so beautiful. And also so small and vulnerable. She was a real person that he and Amy had created. A miracle.

By the evening, all was well with Maya's and Amy's medical checks and so they were allowed to take Maya back to their home.

The Barnes family were thrilled with the new arrival and were anxious to see baby Maya. Ollie and

Maggie came straightaway to the cottage to help out. Amy's parents had been invited to visit but had replied that they were 'very sorry but unable to come just at the moment.' Amy was greatly upset by this reply. They were clearly still furious that she and Dan hadn't married as they had wanted them to. Dan assured her that they would come around one day.

****

When Maya was a week old, Ollie suggested that they should have a get-together at the house to wet little Maya's head. And so the family gathered on the first Saturday in May, when the trees were bursting with green leaves and the garden at the cottage was awash with the vibrant colours of spring flowers.

Matt and Lisa arrived and started chatting to the happy parents. Lisa immediately fell in love with little Maya and asked if she could hold her. She carefully cradled the little bundle in her arms. Matt watched – fascinated and envious. He and Lisa had talked about marriage and he wondered when the time would come for them to start thinking about babies of their own. But he kept the thought to himself. For the moment.

At the end of a shared meal, Ollie made a brief speech.

'You have no idea how much it means to your mum and I to see the whole family together. And especially to welcome lovely little Maya, the first of a new generation of Barnes. So, please raise your glasses for a toast – to Maya, the new generation, and the family.'

Glasses were raised, and the celebrations carried on into the evening as the sun sank into the horizon and the moon rose high above the cottage. The family shared the feeling that this new arrival was the beginning of something special.

All was well.

Chapter 3

An eventful seventeen years passed by after the birth of Maya. Dan and Amy stayed as residents at their home in Birch Cottage as their daughter grew up. Dan continued his employment with the kitchen company. He worked his way up to management level, a job which frequently involved him driving around the Cotswolds to visit customers who wanted to buy smart new kitchens from his employer. Amy had devoted her years to looking after little Maya and making good friends in the village.

But, things had not always been plain sailing for Dan and Amy. A tragedy had unexpectedly struck their family. Two years after Maya's birth, Amy had again become pregnant, but sadly their baby boy was stillborn. And, as a further blow, after the loss and due to medical complications, Amy had to undergo a hysterectomy.

'No womb means no more children, I am afraid. I am so very sorry,' the kind doctor had said.

And so, after this terrible loss, Maya had, even more so, become Dan and Amy's very special treasure. She had inherited Dan's dark hair, dark eyes and slim build. In fact, she had become a strikingly good-looking teenager, who was now in her final year studying for A-Levels at the nearby Milchester Sixth Form College. Her favourite subject was English Literature, which she wanted to study at uni. She had a boyfriend, Luke. Neither Dan nor Amy entirely approved of Luke who they thought was careless and irresponsible. But they knew that Maya was young and they hoped the relationship would fizzle out before it came time for her to leave for university.

Amy and Dan had never married and Amy's Catholic parents had never quite forgiven them, although they adored Maya. But the relationship between Amy and Dan *had* changed. What had begun as a great adventure had eroded away until there was barely anything left. The affection between them had died and, by the time Maya was sixteen, Dan was sleeping in a separate bed. There was an unspoken agreement that they would stay together for Maya but the situation took a toll on Dan. It was a toll that often saw him reaching for a bottle of wine.

Now her daughter was older, Amy had wanted to reclaim some of her own life. And she wanted time away from the cottage. She joined an amateur dramatic group, the Milchester Players, which met regularly in the city just fifteen miles away. She had always, as a student, been interested in the theatre. And she valued the time spent there because of her love of drama. She also made friends with others in the company, including some of the male players who were inevitably attracted by her good looks and lively nature. One in particular, Adam Ashworth, a solicitor, had often bought her drinks in the pub after rehearsals. She admitted to herself that he was very attractive and she couldn't help but think of him often when they were not together.

Ollie and Maggie had, in their retirement, moved to Australia in order to be closer to Ollie's brother – fulfilling a long-held dream to live down-under for a few years. Unfortunately a year later, the family had said goodbye to Maggie who had passed away after a brief battle with cancer. A devastated Ollie remained in Australia but still regularly visited his boys in the UK.

In all the years that had passed since Maya's birth Dan and Matt had remained very close, supporting each other when there were problems and also getting together to enjoy family life. Matt and Lisa had married and welcomed little Sophie who was now six. Dan and Amy would often look after Sophie when Matt and Lisa went on their mountain hiking holidays. Maya loved having a little cousin to care for.

And so, in springtime at Birch Cottage, there was a great buzz of excitement. Matt and Lisa were due to drop off Sophie – a six-year-old bundle of energy. They had again arranged for Sophie to stay at the cottage with Dan and Amy while they were away on one of their popular hiking holidays in Switzerland.

Little Sophie always loved her visits to her Uncle Dan and Auntie Amy, but Maya was her real buddy. Maya would spend lots of time with her, playing games, going on country walks, and telling amazing stories which she made up for her cousin. Maya couldn't wait for Sophie to arrive.

Mid-morning, there was a loud knocking at the cottage door. Maya and Amy rushed to open it. Matt and Lisa were standing in the porch with little Sophie, holding her dolly. Like her mother, Sophie had beautiful blonde hair. Sophie rushed to Maya who held out her arms and gave her a big hug.

'Sophie, you have grown so much,' exclaimed Maya. 'Is that your dolly? She looks just like a princess.'

'Of course. That's why she is called Princess. Look at her lovely hair.'

Sophie looked up at Lisa and asked her pleadingly, 'Mummy, can I go and see Maya's room?'

Maya turned to Lisa. 'Is that OK?'

'Yes, of course,' said Lisa, smiling.

The two girls rushed upstairs, Sophie squealing with excitement.

Amy and Lisa meanwhile went down to the kitchen chatting together, leaving the two brothers in the living room, catching up on family and work. They were identical twins but had spent their lives trying to be and look different. Dan now sported a luxurious black beard in contrast to Matt's shaved face and short, cropped hair.

The ancient grandfather clock in the hallway struck eleven. It was time for Matt and Lisa to leave. After more hugs, the holidaying couple rapidly drove off to catch the plane, their car bumping down the rough and winding lane leading to the main road. Then the front door closed. Maya and Sophie ran back upstairs. And all was quiet at Birch Cottage.

Dan and Amy stood in the hallway looking at each other without saying a word. They could hear Sophie giggling with delight upstairs. But the sound of children playing together made them think of the little baby boy that they had lost so soon. Once upon a time, Dan would have held Amy's hands and pulled her to him in a close hug. Dan knew that any reminder of the loss of their little baby always tore her apart. Instead, they stood apart and in silence.

'We must make the most of Sophie's visit,' he said. 'She loves Maya. They are going to have such a good time together.'

'Let's go to Woodbury Hill tomorrow,' Amy suggested. 'It has such happy memories. I love those remote, wooded areas… you know, where years ago we used to take Maya and lie on the moss, looking up at the trees, watching squirrels jumping from branch to branch. And there were bluebells in full bloom. Yes, it was pure magic.'

'Woodbury Hill it is, Amy,' exclaimed Dan, remembering times spent secretly making love there in their early relationship. He reluctantly put those memories aside. It seemed such a long time ago.

Later in the kitchen, Amy was busy preparing a lunchtime picnic for the trip the next day.

'What about the wine tomorrow, Amy?' Dan asked as he came into the room.

Amy sighed inwardly. Dan always needed to make sure they had wine.

'A bottle of that New Zealand white that you like is in the cooler.'

'Sounds good to me. Is it a sauv blanc?' asked Dan.

'A what?' asked Amy.

'Sauvignon Blanc, of course. That's the name of the grape,' replied Dan grumpily as he made his way to the cooler to fetch the bottle, muttering to himself. Amy watched him go with a sad look on her face.

*****

The next morning dawned with a dramatic sunrise. The sunlight filtered its way like fingers of flame through the trees that surrounded the cottage.

That morning, Matt and Lisa had settled in their Swiss alpine hotel and called in to check on their daughter before they headed out for their first mountain hike of the holiday. Sophie jumped up and down on the sofa, clutching her doll as Dan answered the call. He handed the phone over to his niece.

'Hello Sophie sweetheart, are you having a happy time with Maya? Are you being a good girl?' He could hear Lisa's voice on the other end of the phone.

Sophie held up Princess so that she could speak on the phone.

'Hello, Mummy and Daddy. Princess says hello.'

'That's lovely, my poppet,' replied Lisa. 'Hand the phone back to Uncle Dan now.'

'So what have you got planned for today?' asked Matt as he came on the line.

'A picnic trip up Woodbury Hill,' replied Dan. 'One of Dad's favourites. I am sure you will remember it. Really fab views from the top.'

'Sounds great, Dan. Please, please, keep an eye on our Sophie. She can get overexcited and carried away.'

'Will do... Bye then. Enjoy the mountains,' exclaimed Dan.

Dan drove them from the cottage in his Land Rover, parking at the base of Woodbury Hill. They were soon pacing along a track which wound its way through trees and bracken towards the hill's summit. Halfway up the path, Amy and Sophie were panting, out of breath and tired. The picnic paraphernalia was getting very heavy.

'You are going too fast, Dan,' called out Amy, gasping for breath. 'Sophie's not used to long hikes.'

'I'm so sorry,' replied Dan, also panting. 'I didn't realise. Let's have a few minutes rest… Oh yes, there is a mossy bank here. Let's just sit down for a while and enjoy the view.'

As they sat down Dan told them to listen out for the cuckoos calling and the woodpeckers furiously tapping away at the tree trunks. When they had rested and got their breath back they set off again, taking the long and steep path right to the top of the hill. When they reached its summit, they came to a halt and stood still, amazed by how high they were and the views in all directions. But Maya suddenly looked worried. She had spotted a pool of water not far from where they were standing.

'Oh no!' she exclaimed. 'I hate that horrible pond. Dad, why is it so close to the top of the hill? It looks crazy!'

'It's known locally as the Quarry Pool,' replied Dan. 'It's man-made. It's all that is left of some quarrying activity that happened up here many years ago. It's just one very big pond now.' Dan paused. 'A big green one and not very nice. Totally yucky in fact. So, whatever you do, please do keep well away from it.'

And so they walked on around the summit, following the path as Dan explained to them about its history.

'This hill has a flat summit and used to be a fort in pre-Roman times. You can see two counties from here,' he explained. 'And Milchester is over there in the far distance. You can just about make out the cathedral tower by the river.'

By now they were all getting thirsty and hungry. Dan suggested they stop for the picnic. Amy looked around and found a suitable place on a grassy area to have their picnic, which she then spread out on a rug.

The weather was perfect. A clear blue, cloudless sky stretched from horizon to horizon and they could hear the twittering liquid song of the skylarks flying overhead.

After they had finished their sandwiches and drinks Maya asked if she and Sophie could go off to explore nearby.

'Sophie wants to chase some butterflies,' Maya said, laughing.

'Don't go too far, Maya!' warned Amy. 'And don't be too long. We will need to head back down when we have had a rest.'

'It's OK, Mum,' replied Maya. 'Sophie only wants to chase butterflies.'

The girls soon ran off, leaving Dan and Amy sitting on a rug surrounded by the picnic debris. Amy was preoccupied with brushing and tying back her long red hair and looking at herself critically in a hand mirror. Not bad for someone in her late-thirties, she reckoned. Her thoughts turned to Adam Ashworth again. She secretly very much fancied

Adam, but nothing had happened between them apart from the occasional drink after rehearsals. She often wondered what might happen if she gave in and had an affair with him. She was definitely getting tired of Dan, his drinking and his recent decision to sleep in a separate single bed.

When Amy had finished brushing her hair she put all these thoughts aside and looked down at Dan next to her. He had drunk a lot of the bottle of wine and had inevitably crashed out on the grassy bank and was snoring for England. She guessed she would be the one driving home.

Amy watched the two girls set off and disappear along the path, little Sophie clutching Maya's hand. The girls were such good companions.

The April sun had now reached its zenith and Amy settled down again. The only sounds, apart from song of the skylarks and an occasional cuckoo call, was Dan lying nearby on the grass with his mouth wide open and snoring.

But then, after a while, there was the faint noise of what sounded like screaming in the distance. Amy shook Dan by the shoulder, shouting at him.

'Dan! Dan! Wake up. Can't you hear that noise? I think the girls may be in trouble.'

Dan rubbed his eyes and sat up.

'What the hell is going on?' he asked.

'That's Maya. That's Maya screaming? Come on, Dan… We've got to get to the girls.'

Dan pulled himself together and got to his feet, feeling dizzy. He and Amy set off straightaway, running in the direction of the screaming, which was getting more and more desperate as they got closer to where the noise was coming from – the Quarry Pool.

They found Maya standing by the forbidden pool, waving furiously, the legs of her jeans were sopping wet and covered with green algae.

'Please help,' she cried. 'She's in the water. Sophie is in the water. She was chasing this butterfly and she tripped and fell in. It happened so fast that I didn't see it. I think she had hit her head on one of the stones that are at the edge of the pool. She's in the water. I can't find her. I tried—' Maya's dark eyes were full of terror.

Dan's mind was foggy with wine but he didn't waste a moment.

Instinctively he tore off his shoes and jacket, took in a huge gulp of air, and jumped in, disappearing into the deep water, swimming down and down, thrashing around in the thick weed in the dark pool. In the darkness of the water, he could not see anything. He began to panic. He must find Sophie.

Then, suddenly, he spotted her. Outstretched in front of him. Face down with her hair streaming behind her. Barely moving but slowly sinking. Dan knew that he had to get her out of that water as soon as possible. The water was so very cold and dark, and it was closing in on his chest. He could scarcely breathe. He reached out, taking hold of the precious little girl, holding her up out of the water before carrying her to the edge of the pool.

'I've got her! I've got her!' he shouted over and over again. Amy and Maya stood there, their faces pictures of panic and horror as they saw the state Sophie was in. Amy knelt down and stretched out her arms as Dan lifted the unconscious Sophie towards her. She took the dripping wet bundle from him and clutched it in her arms.

Sophie was, thankfully, still breathing. Amy held her close and started to carry out CPR on the grass next to the pond, using mouth-to-mouth resuscitation and pushing down on Sophie's chest, time and time again. Sophie's face was as white as marble.

Maya meanwhile had immediately grabbed her phone, calling for the emergency services, her fingers fumbling and shaking as she dialed 999.

'What is your emergency?' came the reply almost immediately.

'Please help,' she almost screamed into the phone. 'My cousin has fallen into the pond at the top of Woodbury Hill.'

'Is she still in the water?'

'No. My dad swam in and got her out but she's unconscious.'

'Is she breathing?'

'I don't know! My mum is giving her CPR. Please get help here.'

'What is your name, please?'

'Maya. Maya Barnes. Please get here now.'

'We're dispatching an air ambulance, Maya. Stay on the line.'

Time passed excruciatingly slowly as they waited for help to arrive. Although Amy was getting very tired, she continued to work on Sophie who was still breathing. But only just.

A faint distant buzz in the air grew to a regular beat as the air ambulance helicopter arrived, landing in the open area on the grassy summit of the hill.

Medical crew in bright orange jackets jumped out, carrying backpacks and oxygen cylinders. As the air ambulance landed, Maya noticed that her father was looking pale. In fact, Dan had not spoken since emerging from the pond and handing over the precious wet bundle. He had been feeling increasingly dizzy and lightheaded. He was totally exhausted, dripping wet and shaking with cold and shock.

'Dad,' he heard his daughter ask. 'Dad, are you OK? Dad, can you hear me?'

Then suddenly everything around him started to spin. The trees, the sun and sky in a crazy carousel. He passed out. Swallowed into darkness.

No more than a wet crumpled heap.

Chapter 4

Dan had rescued little Sophie from the dark depths of the Quarry Pool, but was exhausted and traumatised after all his efforts to save the little girl. He had collapsed onto the ground near the pool.

When he eventually came round, he was not in a good state. Maya was leaning over him and he could see paramedics gathered around Sophie and Amy. He was confused and sopping wet, his mop of dark hair, beard and tangled clothes smeared with stinking green algae from the pool. He tried to recall what had happened. He was in a serious state of shock.

'Oh Dad, thank goodness that you are OK. I think you must have fainted or something,' Maya said.

Dan, who was now fully conscious of what was happening, spluttered: 'Is Sophie all right?'

'I don't know,' replied Maya. 'The paramedics are here now. They're helping her.'

'Yes, yes, I can see now. I found her under all that slime in the water.'

'You rescued her, Dad.' Maya was getting very concerned about her father's odd behaviour. 'You seem so cold and shivery. I'm going to ask a paramedic to look at you, too.'

Maya ran to fetch one of the paramedic team before she made her way back to their picnic site, picked up a blanket and returned to drape it around her father's shoulders. It had been a long day for him and it was now turning into a nightmare. Maya made her way back over to where her mother was standing next to the medical team working on Sophie. One of the crew, who seemed to be the one in charge, spoke to Amy and Maya.

'My name is Neeta. I have some questions about the situation. First of all: how long was Sophie in the water?'

Amy was unsure. She turned to Maya.

'Not sure,' replied a confused Maya. 'A few minutes. Not long. Everything is a bit of a blur. My dad went into the water to get her out.' She paused and then exclaimed, 'Oh my God. This is all my fault. I am so sorry. I was supposed to be looking after her.' Maya burst into tears. It was all too much.

'It's OK, Maya, it's not your fault,' said Amy.

'I am OK,' sobbed Maya. 'Just so worried about our little Sophie.'

Neeta, who was very anxious to find out the facts of the incident interrupted to gather vital information.

'Was Sophie breathing when she came out of the water?' asked Neeta.

'Barely but I know my CPR and I managed to get her breath back,' Amy confirmed.

'Just to get things straight… you are Sophie's mother?'

Amy looked confused. 'No! I'm her aunt. My name is Amy. Sophie is staying with us while her parents are away on holiday.'

'Sorry! OK, then. I know that this will all be very distressing for you, but we will be taking Sophie to hospital in the helicopter for further treatment. I suggest that one of you comes with us. Where is your vehicle parked?'

'My dad went into the water and he should probably be checked out, too. Can you take him?'

'Yes. It will help when Sophie regains consciousness. She will need to see a familiar face as otherwise everything will be completely strange and frightening for her.'

'Maya, you and I can get back down the hill and head to the hospital in the car,' suggested Amy.

'Your daughter may need looking after after all the trauma she has been through. Is that her dad sitting over there, wrapped up in a blanket?' Neeta asked.

'Yes, that's Dan, my partner and Sophie's uncle.'

Amy called Dan over. His clothes were still sopping wet and he was looking very pale. Neeta said to him in a quiet and comforting voice:

'You look very cold, Dan. You did a great job rescuing Sophie. Were you in the water for a long time?'

It was Dan's turn to look confused by all these questions before he answered, 'I'm sorry. I don't really know. It took maybe a couple of minutes to find Sophie. I can't really remember. I think I passed out after I got her out of the water.'

'Well, we should take you in the helicopter with Sophie, and get you checked out. We have towels and more blankets to warm you up.'

Dan nodded his head. But he still seemed rather confused.

'But how are you getting to hospital?' he asked Amy. 'And what about Maya?'

'We'll get the car and see you there,' said Amy.

'Come on, Dan,' Neeta said as her colleagues lifted Sophie's small, limp body onto a stretcher. 'We are about to take off. Let's get Sophie to hospital.'

Crows were circling, cawing loudly while Amy and Maya stood watching the helicopter leave. Amy's arm was around Maya's shoulders. The throbbing sound of the helicopter slowly died away as it headed off into the distance. Then, all was silent as the crows returned to their trees.

In the helicopter Neeta checked Dan's vital signs. A screen had been put up between him and his niece but he could hear the medics continuing to work on Sophie.

'Is she going to be OK?' he asked. Neeta told Dan that the water in the pool would have been bitterly cold and very dangerous. That was why Sophie was very white. They needed to get her breathing regulated and her circulation going. And very soon.

Dan tried to calm himself by looking out of the helicopter window, watching Cotswold villages passing below, their churches and clusters of honey-coloured stone cottages dotted among the trees like toy buildings. He thought he could see Birch Cottage tucked away among the trees, but he was still confused and felt tearful. Eventually the winding River Avon and the tower of Milchester Cathedral came into sight.

The helicopter circled round and approached the

roof of the city hospital. It all seemed like a nightmare to Dan. Was all this really happening? He fumbled in his pocket for his phone but found it missing. He reckoned that it must be on the picnic blanket back at the hill. And what would he tell Matt and Lisa? How was he going to be able to explain it all to them? And he couldn't contemplate what would happen if Sophie didn't make it.

There was a gentle bump as the helicopter landed. They were met by the emergency team who took Sophie straight off to the resuscitation unit. They had no time to lose.

****

Meanwhile, back at Woodbury Hill, Amy and Maya gathered the remains of the picnic. Maya pocketed her father's phone which she'd found lying next to the half empty bottle of wine. And she carefully picked up Sophie's doll, Princess. Sophie would want her when she woke up. They stumbled back down the hill to the car, passing on their way the dreaded pond. They did their best to look the other way. After what had seemed like an eternity they reached the car park, totally exhausted.

'We need to get to Milchester Hospital,' Maya said, 'and as soon as possible. But are you OK to drive, Mum? Are you absolutely sure?'

'Yep. Sure. I'm OK now,' she paused. 'Well, sort of. To be honest I'm in a real mess. But I can still drive a car.'

As they set off in the car Maya texted Luke, her boyfriend:

> 'Oh my God. You will never guess what has happened. I was looking after my little cousin Sophie and she fell in that awful pond up on Woodbury Hill. We are taking her to hospital right now! I need you! Please!

Maya spent most of the remaining journey looking out of the car window and waiting for a reply that didn't come.

When they reached the hospital they passed through swing doors into a large entrance hall and followed the signs to Accident and Emergency. They spoke to a pleasant and helpful young nurse at the reception desk wearing a badge with the name Emma on it.

Amy explained what had happened. 'We're here to see Sophie Barnes. She has been brought here by air ambulance along with my partner.'

Emma started to scroll through her computer screen.

Amy continued, 'She fell in a pond and my partner pulled her out. Is there any news? Is she OK? Can we see her?'

'Please come this way,' Emma said, her face serious. 'Your partner is through here. He's waiting to see Doctor Merrick.

Amy and Maya were led to a side room with comfy chairs and pictures of the sea on the wall. Dan was already there, sitting down, looking haggard and broken. Sitting opposite him was Doctor Merrick.

'Please, come in and sit down,' the doctor said. Amy had a sudden sense of dread. What was happening?

'I am afraid we did everything we could but we lost Sophie half an hour ago,' said the doctor. Dan felt the ceilings and the walls crash in on him and barely heard what the doctor said next. 'I'm afraid that Sophie suffered from cold water shock when she hit the water. The human body can react strongly to a sharp shock of cold water. A lot of water is taken in during this shock. Whilst Sophie was in the water for only a matter of minutes, during that time she had inhaled a lot of water into her lungs. And that water was extremely cold. It led to a great deal of stress on her heart and I am afraid she had a cardiac attack. We did all we could to resuscitate her. I am so very sorry for your loss.'

'She's gone, Dan, the little poppet is gone,' Amy shrieked in horror. 'Gone forever. What have we done? Oh my God! Such a sweet girl. We were supposed to look after her. How the hell am I going to tell Lisa that her little girl is dead?'

Maya looked down at her lap. She still carried Sophie's doll, Princess. Instead of handing it to her smiling cousin in a hospital bed, she now held it in trembling hands knowing that she would never see her again.

Dan felt heavy with grief and shock as he realised that he would have to tell his brother – that his daughter was dead. He felt he was being pulled apart at the thought of it. The room fell silent. Nobody spoke.

Doctor Merrick cleared his throat then raised the issue that Dan was already dreading.

'I understand that Sophie's parents are abroad. We need to inform them.'

'I— I'll tell my brother,' Dan stammered. 'I need to tell my brother. I have to tell him myself.' Maya fumbled in her pocket and handed her father his phone. His hand shaking, Dan made a call to Matt.

The line went straight to voicemail. Matt must be out of range, he thought.

'This is Matt Barnes. I am sorry I cannot answer the phone at the moment. Please leave me a message and I'll get back to you.'

'Matt. Call me as soon as you can. It's urgent,' Dan's voice was becoming more and more croaky as he ended the call.

'Sorry, so what happens now?' Dan asked the doctor. 'What happens when my brother and his wife get back to the UK? Will they be able to see her?'

'Of course they will,' Doctor Merrick replied. 'Sophie's body will remain with us here in the hospital until they return. In any event, we will need to see them to talk about Sophie and what has happened. And we have already notified the police. They will want to speak with you. And a post-mortem will be carried out to confirm the nature and cause of the death.'

'The police? But why?' asked Dan, visibly shocked.

'I am afraid it's standard practice in cases of sudden accidental death of a child.'

Doctor Merrick looked around at the stunned and distressed family.

'I am so sorry for you all. Are there any more questions?' There was a shaking of heads. Doctor Merrick continued, 'I appreciate it is a very difficult time. I really do feel for you all. Can we get your contact details at reception before you leave the hospital.'

'Yes, I'll leave all our details,' replied Amy.

'Can I—' Maya stammered. 'Can I leave Princess?' She held up the little doll. 'It's Sophie's doll. Princess. She would want her doll to be with her.'

Doctor Merrick smiled kindly and took the doll from Maya.

'That's a lovely idea,' she said. 'I'll make sure one of the nurses takes Princess to Sophie.'

Dan, Amy and Maya were then ushered out of the hospital. Nobody spoke as they piled into Dan's Land Rover and drove off into the dark night. All three remained deep in thought on the journey.

After what seemed to be an interminable time on the road they reached their home and heard the characteristic crunch of car wheels on the gravel drive of Birch Cottage. It was a cold dark night. Phones were put away and the three exhausted passengers made their way to the front door.

Inside, Dan and Amy both watched as Maya rapidly disappeared upstairs, stifling sobs.

'Is she going to be alright, Amy?' asked Dan anxiously.

'She is very shocked and traumatised,' replied Amy. 'Leave her for a moment. Anyway, I think you ought to get out of those clothes, Dan.'

'Yes, I suppose so.' Dan felt numb.

Standing under the hot stream of water from the shower, Dan felt the weight of what had happened on him. He closed his eyes but all he saw was Sophie's little body floating in that dreadful green water. How could he let this happen? How was he going to tell his brother. He checked his phone as he dried himself. There was still no response from his brother.

After his shower Dan returned to the kitchen where Amy was sitting at the table, her head in her hands. He shoved his clothes into the bin. There was no point in trying to wash the green water off them and he couldn't stand looking at them.

'Any sign of Maya coming down?' she asked.

'No, she's still upstairs. I checked on her and she's just crying. She really has been through it today. I am sure she has been messaging that boy, Luke, again. So… what are you going to say when Matt calls back?'

'I have no idea,' replied Dan, his feelings of guilt overwhelming him. He really couldn't think straight. How was he going to break the news to Matt and Lisa?

The hours and minutes waiting for Dan's phone to ring dragged slowly by. Maya was up in her room and showed no sign of wanting to join Amy and Dan, who were quietly sitting downstairs in silence waiting for the phone to ring. Scarcely a word passed between them as the clock ticked slowly onwards. A cold, stressful atmosphere pervaded Birch Cottage.

'Why on earth did you allow Maya to take Sophie down to that area by the pond?' Dan asked Amy, breaking the silence. 'You know how dangerous it can be. You heard me say so.'

'But you were the one who passed out from half a bottle of wine… again,' she replied, accusingly.

Silence enveloped them again. This war of words was hurting them both.

'I'm going upstairs,' Amy announced. She disappeared through the door and up to her room. Dan poured himself a large whisky and sat back down at the table. Shortly afterwards, his phone rang. It was his brother. Dan answered the phone.

43

Chapter 5

Earlier that dreadful day, Matt and Lisa had stood gazing at the beautiful view from the top of the Swiss mountain they had just climbed. They were in high spirits, having enjoyed a beautiful and inspiring walk.

They were discussing holidays for next year. Would they come back to Wengwald?

'I've had a brilliant idea,' Matt said, a serious look on his face.

'Yes?' Lisa asked anxiously. She was used to Matt's 'ideas' which sometimes sadly ended in failure.

'So, why don't we ask Dan, Amy and maybe Maya to join us for the next hiking trip? Sophie will be old enough to manage the hikes next year.'

'I am not sure whether that will work,' replied Lisa, shaking her head. 'Dan likes his booze too much these days.'

Matt sighed. 'Now that's not fair, Lisa. Come on now. But... perhaps you're right and it is not such a good idea to have him with us. We could still bring Sophie next year, though. She'll love it. Anyway, where would you like to go tomorrow?'

'I don't mind, Matt. You are my guide.' Lisa was relieved that Matt wasn't going to pursue the idea of bringing their in-laws next year.

'How about taking the mountain train up to the base of the Eiger mountain and walking back down from there? There is a good path down and the views are breathtaking.'

'Sounds great to me,' replied Lisa. 'And the forecast is promising. It says sunshine for most of the day.'

'It's getting late now. Shall we head back to the hotel? We can check in with Birch Cottage and Sophie and then go for dinner.'

She smiled as she stretched out and held her husband's hand.

'And maybe we could try that brandy you bought in the village earlier,' Lisa gave him a wicked grin. 'And then we could get to bed really early? You never know, we might be able to try again for a little sister for Sophie this month.' Matt smiled.

The couple got ready to head back. Lisa grasped Matt's hand as they headed down the mountain He loved these holidays and he hoped one day it would be the three of them or even four of them.

As they neared the hotel, Matt's phone pinged as it picked up the signal. He grabbed it and stared at the screen. He signalled for Lisa to slow down as he listened to the message received. It was his brother on the line and he sounded very worried. Lisa immediately came to a halt, wondering what had happened.

'What is it?' Lisa asked anxiously. 'It's not about Sophie, is it? Oh God, I hope not!'

'It's Dan,' Matt said, furiously dialling his

brother's number. 'Something has happened.'

'What? Oh no!' Lisa grabbed Matt's arm as he waited for his brother to answer.

'Matt.'

'Dan, I got your message. We only just got a signal back. What has happened? Is Sophie OK?'

Back at Birch Cottage, Dan hesitated, wondering how on earth he was going to be able to tell his brother what had happened.

'Dan? What's happened?' he asked. 'Hang on, Lisa is here too, I'm putting you on speaker phone so she can join in the call.'

Dan paused and then, speaking slowly and quietly, said, 'It's Sophie. There's been an accident.'

'Oh my God! What has happened? Is she OK?' Lisa exclaimed.

'We went up to Woodbury Hill today, like we told you—'

'But what has happened to my daughter?' Lisa almost screamed.

'I'm so sorry. I am afraid that Sophie had an accident and fell into the pond, and she went under the water. She must have hit her head.' Dan paused. There was a cold silence from Matt and Lisa. Dan continued. 'I dived in after her and managed to get her to the surface. She was still breathing when I carried her out of the pool and Amy performed First Aid on her. We called an ambulance and they were there within minutes.' Matt and Lisa were still silent on the end of the phone, holding their breath and dreading the worst.

'We thought she'd pull through but... I'm so sorry, Matt. I don't know how to say it.'

There was no reply from Matt or Lisa. They were stunned. Lost for words.

'I don't know what to say,' Dan continued. 'I am so very sorry. She's – her body – she is still at the hospital. They're waiting for you to get back. And the police said they will speak to us. Matt… are you still there?'

'We'll be on the first plane home,' Matt said in a flat voice before he terminated the call. He could not face taking the conversation any further. Nothing more could be said. He turned off his phone and put his arm around Lisa. They clung together, standing outside their beautiful Swiss hotel.

Lisa eventually cried 'It's our child! Gone! Gone forever! Our only child! Dear God! I just can't believe it! I've got to get to her, Matt. Please, please can we go home?'

Matt held her tight and tried to calm her sobbing. All the while the tears were streaming down his own face. He spoke to her with desperation in his voice, 'I really cannot believe it. How can this have possibly happened? How could my brother allow this to happen? Oh my God! Why wasn't he watching her?'

It was now evening but they could not contemplate sleep and so Matt busied himself organising a flight home. The first one available was the next morning. He sent a very brief text message to Dan telling him they were on the way.

Dan messaged back:

> 'Matt, please. I am so sorry. Please call me when you get back. I can come to the hospital with you.'

'Huh,' snorted Matt, showing the message to Lisa. 'No way. What the hell were they playing at? They should have been looking after her.'

Lisa did not answer. She was choking back tears and slowly packing up their belongings.

Matt and Lisa did not sleep during the remainder of that dark night. In the early hours they watched, through the window, the faint light of dawn appearing over the mountains, eventually turning the sky a vivid pink over the snow-capped peaks. They instinctively knew, without saying a word to each other, that Sophie would have loved to have seen those vivid colours and majestic mountains. But now, that would never ever happen. A door had been slammed shut, leaving them in darkness.

****

Matt and Lisa left the hotel in the early hours and took a taxi to the train station. They were soon on the train, leaving the mountains behind them and rattling along towards Zurich Airport. When they eventually reached the air terminal they were greeted by overhead information boards announcing that the Bristol flight had been delayed by an hour.

'Bloody hell!' complained a frustrated Matt as they settled down on the airport seats waiting for their flight to be called. Lisa said nothing. There was nothing further to say.

After a long wait, their flight was called to the gate and they boarded. Sleep on the plane was impossible. And they didn't speak. They both stared into the middle distance, saying nothing. The announcement was eventually made that the plane would land in ten minutes.

'Where's the car, Matt?' asked an exasperated Lisa once they had landed and reclaimed their luggage. But Matt was in such a state that he could not remember where it was parked. He was normally well-organised when it came to travel arrangements but now he seemed to have lost his sense of direction, as well as his temper. And now the car.

Lisa muttered a variety of expletives as they struggled with their luggage through the car parks, scanning the rows of cars. Eventually they located the car. But the first thing they saw when they opened the rear door was Sophie's child seat.

Lisa cried out, 'Oh my God, help me. I just can't take this.'

Matt pulled Lisa close to him and they stood quietly for a few minutes. No words could comfort them. Eventually, they climbed into the car, Matt stirred the engine into action and they set off for Milchester Hospital, sixty miles away.

Half an hour later of fast driving they spotted a message board: QUEUE AHEAD. ACCIDENT. EXPECT DELAYS.

'Just what we need,' muttered Matt angrily. Neither of them was looking forward to what awaited them at the hospital, but they both wanted to get there as fast as possible. They wanted to get to their little girl.

After a long and frustrating journey the exhausted couple eventually reached the motorway turn-off to Milchester. Not another word was spoken as they made their way through the Milchester suburbs and finally reached their destination.

Matt put his arm around Lisa's shoulders as they

walked up to the hospital building. Everything seemed so unreal, just like a bad dream. Matt spoke to the receptionist, who looked sympathetic and then made a phone call and asked them to take a seat. The reception area was busy and noisy with children running around and shrieking.

After a while they were approached by another nurse.

'Mr and Mrs Barnes?'

'Yes, that's us,' said Matt as they stood up.

'I'm so sorry for your loss. Your brother formally identified your daughter, Mr Barnes. But you can see her, if that is what you want to do.'

Lisa and Matt both nodded.

They were taken down a series of corridors and then into a small room dominated by a trolley covered by a white sheet.

'Again, I'm so sorry for your loss,' the nurse said quietly.

Matt and Lisa were both nodding solemnly as the nurse delicately and slowly pulled back the white sheet to reveal Sophie's face. Lisa gasped and cried out aloud. Resting next to her was her doll, Princess.

'My baby! Our little angel! Look at her, Matt. She's gone.'

Sophie looked so very normal apart from the cold whiteness of her skin. Their little girl could have been asleep. Her blue eyes were closed and her long blonde hair had been carefully brushed. She looked like an angel.

'Can I... can I touch her?' Lisa was finding it difficult to speak.

'Yes,' said the nurse, who was expecting the question. 'You may touch her. Of course.'

Lisa reached out to touch her daughter, and gently stroked her cold white cheeks, her hair and then her face. Matt then passed his hand delicately through her hair and over her cold pallid skin. The Sophie whom they loved so very much had been taken away. It was a heart-wrenching and tearful farewell. There was nothing they could say as they were shown out of the room by the nurse. All they could do was to hug and hold hands.

Half an hour later, Matt and Lisa left in a dazed state. They made their way back to their parked car.

'Let's get home,' said Matt. 'We will need to find out from Dan and Amy exactly what happened to Sophie. But not now. I really don't want to speak to them… not yet anyway.'

Lisa nodded her head. 'Yes. Absolutely,' she said, with feeling as Matt started the car's engine. They dreaded the thought of getting back to their silent house and all the reminders of their precious little daughter Sophie. How would they manage to cope with it all?

Chapter 6

A week had passed since Sophie's death. Dan had tried to contact his brother Matt repeatedly but neither Matt or Lisa had taken any of his calls. He had also sent many messages but there had been no response from his brother. Not a word.

It was another long week later that Dan and Amy received a formal notification of Sophie's funeral. It was to take place in a week's time in Bristol, near where Matt and Lisa lived. There was no personal message from them, just a plain printed card giving details of the crematorium, the time of the funeral service and an invitation to refreshments afterwards at the nearby community centre.

'Hmmm,' grunted Dan, 'this is all a bit impersonal. But I am not really surprised. They must be going through hell and back. Maybe when I see Matt face-to-face we can hopefully be able to talk together. I really do need to tell him how sorry I am.'

'I think that might be difficult for them at the funeral, Dan,' replied Amy. 'You might just need to give Matt some time.'

Dan decided to write a personal letter of condolence to Matt and Lisa. He sent the letter. But there was still no reply.

****

Time passed by slowly and inevitably until the day of the funeral. It was a drab Monday and rain fell from a dark sky as the procession of friends and relatives entered the crematorium, shaking their umbrellas as they went in. A low buzz of conversation pervaded the chapel as old friends and relatives consoled each other. Dan, Amy and Maya made their way to the front row where Dan hoped he would see his brother. It was not long before he saw him, standing beside his wife and speaking with another couple. They were nodding but Lisa had tears on her cheeks. Matt glanced up and for a moment, his eyes caught his brother's. It was only for a second but Dan felt a cold chill from his brother's look before Matt turned deliberately away again.

Feeling heavy with grief and guilt, Dan ushered Amy and Maya into a row a few back from the front where Dan and Lisa were seated. As they sat down, Dan felt sorry that his father hadn't been able to attend. Ollie was not well and was in hospital having blood tests. The loss of his much-loved wife, Maggie still weighed heavily on him and he had been inconsolable to hear what had happened to his granddaughter. His doctor had suggested that it would be too much of a trauma for him to make the long journey home whilst he was in such a state.

The room fell silent at the sound of the doors opening. Everybody turned to see the undertakers carry into the chapel a small white coffin smothered with spring flowers, including bunches of Sophie's favourite – buttercups. Placed in the middle of this golden display was the doll, Princess. It brought tears to Dan's eyes.

The organ started playing as the priest entered the chapel and the congregation stood up. The priest was a kindly man who brought a human warmth to the ceremony.

'We are here today,' he began, looking around at the congregation, 'to say farewell to beautiful little Sophie who has been sadly taken away from us all. Let us now have a quiet minute to remember her.'

There was total silence in the chapel for a moment.

The priest then continued, 'Our service starts with the hymn – "All things bright and beautiful" – a hymn that Sophie often sang at school. I hope it will remind us of the bright and beautiful little girl that she was.'

And so the service continued until it was the time for the eulogy, given by Matt. He recounted his treasured memories of Sophie, who he described as a very happy and selfless child. He finally read a short poem which he wanted to include in this part of the service.

'The world may never notice if a buttercup does not bloom,
The road is rough that leads to the damp dark tomb,
The little flower we all adored was swiftly here and gone,

But the face we loved is a golden light that still shines on and on…'

At this point Matt stopped and tried to suppress his tears. He looked around at the congregation – making special effort not to lock eyes with his brother – then pulled out a handkerchief, wiped his eyes and carried on, his voice choking.

'But if our arms are sadly empty,

As we love and miss her so,

Her golden laughter still stays in our minds,

Wherever we may go.'

As Matt sat back down, the congregation remained totally silent, greatly moved by the poem.

It was now the time for the coffin to be committed to the flames. There was a hush in the chapel as the flower-covered coffin disappeared, sliding through the curtains. There was a terrible finality in the way that Sophie's body was to leave the world.

Amy held Maya's hand as the curtains closed on the tiny coffin. Both of them were very distressed and Dan was wiping his eyes with his handkerchief. He couldn't stop picturing Sophie's body floating in that dark water.

The priest concluded with prayers and an invitation for the congregation to join Matt and Lisa for refreshments at the community centre, just down the road. The congregation slowly filed out of the crematorium into an open area of trees and flowers. Groups of friends and relatives stood chatting. The rain clouds had dispersed and bright warm sunshine gave its benediction – a final blessing on the scene.

Dan, Amy and Maya joined the crowd outside and saw that Matt and Lisa were surrounded by friends and in deep conversation. Dan still badly wanted to speak to Matt.

'It was all my fault,' said Maya, suddenly.

'It was *not* your fault,' Amy responded, adamantly, before pulling her daughter into her arms. Maya began to cry. She had never attended a funeral before. Dan had travelled to Australia for his mother's funeral alone, thinking it would be better for his daughter to focus on her schoolwork and say goodbye to her grandmother in her own personal way. Maya was now distraught by what she had just experienced. It was all the more traumatic because it had been for her own young cousin who was just six years old. She had spent so many happy times with little Sophie, and she was now desperately upset. She began to sob and beg Dan and Amy to take her home.

'Can we go home now? I just cannot face seeing all these people. I know that it was my fault that Sophie drowned. I am never ever going to get over this. Please can we leave this place? Right now. I really, really want to go home.'

Dan and Amy looked at each other. No further words were necessary. Dan was still desperate to speak to his brother but his daughter needed him first. They were going straight back. They had to get Maya home.

'Maya, it was just a terrible accident. You mustn't blame yourself,' he said, keenly aware of his own crippling guilt over what had happened to Sophie.

Maya shook her head vigorously. 'But I was supposed to be looking after her,' she sobbed.

'And you did, you called to us and we came. And she was still alive and breathing when she came out of the water. Remember?' replied Dan emphatically.

But Maya could not be consoled. They turned and walked towards the car. Dan slowed and glanced back at his brother but Matt didn't look his way. They got into the car and began the journey back home. Maya eventually stopped crying and a terrible silence pervaded the car. Dan tried to focus on his driving but the images of his niece floating in the dark water, then being carried on a stretcher into the helicopter and the sight of Princess sitting on top of her little white coffin would not go away. What had happened wasn't Maya's fault. *It was his fault.*

As soon as they got into the cottage Maya rushed upstairs to her bedroom where she collapsed, exhausted, onto her bed. She phoned her boyfriend Luke. There was no answer so she left a garbled voicemail.

'Luke, I need to talk. This is getting too much. I can't stand it all. I know it was my fault that Sophie drowned. Mum and Dad say that's not true. I need you, Luke. I want you to be with me and tell me that I am not going mad.'

Dan and Amy were meanwhile sitting downstairs at the kitchen table, listening to the muffled sounds of Maya's outpouring of despair. Dan poured a glass of wine for Amy and a larger glass for himself. He couldn't help but note Amy's disapproving look.

'It really was a very emotional service,' commented Amy. 'That was a powerful poem that Matt read. So descriptive. And also so personal. I hadn't heard it before. Where did it come from?'

'No idea. As you say, it was so personal and appropriate for poor little Sophie.'

'It was lovely,' replied Amy. '

'But,' said Dan, 'also seeing her doll Princess on the coffin was heartbreaking. It doesn't seem right. I just can't imagine what Matt and Lisa were faced with – going back to their home and seeing Sophie's toys, her bedroom and her school uniform. It must have been so quiet. Horribly so.'

They sat in silence for some time. Eventually Amy stood up and yawned.

'I think it is time for bed now. Maya is already upstairs, no doubt still talking to that boyfriend. You heading up too?'

'In a while,' Dan said, pouring another glass of wine.

Amy sighed and left him to it. Dan watched her leave, wishing they still had the sort of relationship where he could open up to her. He felt as if he was going to explode with pain and guilt. Dan sipped at the wine until it was gone. The wine had made his mind fuzzy and it had become easier to block out the memory of his brother's cold stare. But he still kept circling around to the same conclusion. *It was his fault.*

All was quiet outside, apart from an owl hooting in the woods and a strong wind picking up and creaking the branches of the trees. Eventually, fuddled from his wine, Dan stumbled up the stairs and fell into the bed in the spare room that he now slept in. On his own. As he slept, he had a vivid dream. He was trapped in a dark place underwater. A small white coffin drifted towards him and, as it did, the lid began to open. Sophie emerged with outspread arms and long fair hair trailing in the water behind her. A white angel.

He woke with a start, sweating and gasping for breath. It had all been so real. He lay quietly in bed for a while. He was a mental wreck.

****

The next morning Dan woke up to find that Amy was in the kitchen.

'Bloody hell, Dan. I could hear you down the hall last night. Whatever possessed you?' she asked. 'You kept shouting out in your sleep.'

'Yeah, sorry,' replied Dan. 'Had a nightmare. What else do you expect though? I have been to hell and back, and I was dreaming about Sophie. It has been so traumatic.'

Amy looked thoughtful. 'I think I understand now. It'll take time. Oh my God, look at the time. I am supposed to be taking Maya into college today. We're going to be late.'

She called upstairs to tell Maya to hurry up. She soon came downstairs, ready to go. Maya was anxious to get to the college on time. She, too, had experienced a bad night and needed to return to normality and talk to normal people. They jumped into the car, Amy put her foot down and flew down the lane to the main road.

Dan was left home alone. In total silence. He wanted to contact his father and find out how his visit to the hospital had gone and then to talk to him about all that had happened at the funeral. He thought that maybe he would call him later.

****

The week that followed was a difficult one for Maya. She tried to return to normal life but could not put aside her thoughts about the funeral and her feelings of guilt over Sophie's death. On Friday she returned home from college in floods of tears. Her mother was home and Amy gave her a big hug and sat her down in the kitchen.

'Of course you feel sad. It's part of the grieving process to feel this way, my love,' Amy assured her.

'It's not just about feeling sad, Mum,' Maya said. 'I can't stop reliving it and wondering if I could have saved her if I'd just gone a little further into the water to try and get her myself.'

'Maya!' exclaimed Amy, 'Your father had to dive deep into that water to rescue her. If you'd gone in any further, you could have drowned too and—' Amy paused, shaken with the idea that something could have happened to Maya. 'And I don't know what I would have done if that happened.' Amy fell silent. Shocked by her own reaction to the thought of Maya getting hurt, she was suddenly thinking about Lisa and Matt and how they were coping.

'It's not just that, though.' Maya said. 'I feel selfish for feeling like this but... It's Luke. I could really do with his support right now. I just wish he was different. He can be so stupid and thoughtless and hurtful.'

'So, what's he done this time?' Amy was getting very annoyed with this boyfriend who had developed something of a record of upsetting Maya and letting her down.

'He says he's sick of me talking about what happened. He says I should get over it. It's only been a few weeks – how can I get over it? He says I'm no fun because I'm always crying.'

'I am so sorry, darling. I really wonder about that Luke sometimes. You deserve someone much better, my love.' Amy passed a tissue to Maya, who wiped her eyes and blew her nose.

'But I really care about him, Mum,' Maya sobbed again. 'I think… I think I might be in love with him.'

Amy sighed. 'I know you have strong feelings for him,' she said, slowly. 'But Luke doesn't seem to give a lot of thought to your feelings.'

Maya knew that what her mother was saying was true, but she could stand no more. She stood up from the table and rushed up to her bedroom. Inconsolable.

Later, in the evening, Dan returned from a long day driving to visit a client in Oxford. Maya was still in her room. She hadn't even come down to get something to eat.

'Is it about Sophie?' he asked Amy.

'It's more than that,' Amy answered. 'That Luke. He's always trouble and no good for her.'

'So what's he done now?'

'Just been thoughtless and hurtful. She thinks she's in love with him, though. I tried to talk to her, but there didn't seem to be much I could do to help. She kept bursting into tears.'

Dan marched out of the room, muttering and swearing about 'that idiot Luke'. He went upstairs, knocked on Maya's door and heard her invite him in. She was lying on her bed and so he perched on the edge and turned to face her.

'Sorry you have had such a bad day. Mum said that things are getting on top of you.'

'Yeah,' replied Maya. 'They sure are. And Luke has not made things any better. He just wants my attention on him all the time.'

Dan hated to see her in such a mess. He knew it was his job to make her feel safe, but also to cheer her up. And so they sat chatting together in her bedroom and Dan worked his magic.

'Listen, Maya, you will soon be at uni. You will have a great time there studying and meeting all sorts of people on your own wavelength. Maybe you might move on from Luke and from your life here?'

'But I think I love him, Dad. And besides, I will have to pass my exams first, Dad. I need to get my grades. And I'm finding it so hard to concentrate at the moment.'

'Don't worry,' replied Dan. 'You will get good grades. I am sure of that. You have a Barnes brain in your head. Just remember that.' Maya sat up and threw her arms around her father. Dan held her for a moment and then then drew back and looked straight into her dark eyes. 'Also, you are a beautiful girl and will have all the boys after you. No problem there.'

Dan went downstairs and rejoined Amy, who was watching TV whilst dinner cooked in the oven. The program involved a group of young men who were competing to partner one of a group of very attractive women at a Caribbean holiday resort. Amy suggested that she should turn the TV off, but Dan was intrigued by the idea. He wondered how he would score in a situation like that. He was heading for his thirty-ninth birthday, though. Not a hope in hell, he reckoned.

****

The next day Dan and Amy were sitting at the kitchen table after supper, going through their diaries. They needed to coordinate who was dropping Maya at college for her exams and her various social engagements. Dan reminded her about a business trip he would be taking the following week. It would stretch into the weekend, he told her.

'The company is throwing a major event for employees next weekend. It will be held at the main company headquarters in Frankfurt. So, I'll be there from Saturday through to Monday.'

'All weekend? What for?' asked a suspicious Amy.

'Well, it's a celebration of twenty years of profitable trading by Leichmatic. Basically it is a big booze-up for all the German branches and they've invited the UK team over too.'

Amy sighed. Dan paused, expecting her to ask if she could come as well, but she said nothing. She already had something else in her diary.

'Well, Maya is staying with a friend that weekend but I have plans. The Milchester Players have a rehearsal and then we're going for drinks. The week after we're workshopping some love poetry. You know... Shakespeare, Donne, Tennyson, Shelley and all that lot.'

'Huh?' Dan looked confused.

'You know perfectly well what I am talking about, Dan.'

'Oh yes. That poetic lot. Sorry. Not up my street I'm afraid.'

Amy shook her head and snapped her diary shut.

'So we are both sorted for that weekend are we? You're off to Germany to live it up and I'll be here with my friends. And no doubt you hope there will be some attractive German women in the company to look after you and all your possible needs.'

Dan ignored Amy's pointed comments. But he quietly wondered whether she was also thinking about her needs and who would satisfy them. The two of them hadn't slept together for more than a year now.

'Oh,' he added, 'and I've got a meeting with someone from head office on Monday before I fly home. Not sure what it's about but I'll find out.'

There was no response from Amy who had got up and began to tidy the kitchen. Dan had decided that the time had come to put an end to the conversation. He got up from the table and walked out of the room.

Dan's weekend in Frankfurt did not surprise or worry Amy. She had been thinking only that morning about her upcoming weekend with her acting friends. It would be a welcome relief after all the trauma they had been through. And she would get to spend time with Adam Ashworth. Amy enjoyed flirting with him. And he enjoyed flirting with her, too, she reckoned. She understood, only too well, that her relationship with Dan was becoming less and less sustainable as time moved on. They were drifting further and further away from each other.

Chapter 7

The morning of his German trip arrived abruptly for Dan: the alarm on his phone roused him from his dreams, telling him that it was six o'clock in the morning and he needed to get a move on. A drive to Birmingham Airport lay ahead, followed by a late morning flight to Frankfurt.

After taking a shower he looked at himself critically in the bathroom mirror. He thought about Amy's comment about attractive German women he might encounter on this trip. He reckoned he looked fairly acceptable for his age. He was almost forty but he still had the typical Barnes' slim build, muscular physique and dark hair – although he had recently put on some weight around the waistline area. Amy had told him it was because he drank too much. He also insisted on sporting the dark beard which Amy also did not like. He reckoned it gave him an air of gravitas and had told Amy that he thought it made him look serious and dignified. Amy had replied that it made him look like a tramp.

As he was getting dressed, Dan could hear the

raised voices of Amy and Maya having a heated discussion in the kitchen.

'For God's sake, Mum, can't you just take me today? The basketball match I am playing in is very important.'

'Look, Maya, I do actually have a life aside from ferrying you around. It's not my fault that boyfriend of yours is too hungover to take you as he promised.'

'Come on, Mum, give me a break. How else can I get to the match today? Walk there, maybe? Or hitchhike with some dodgy looking man.'

'Fine,' Amy sighed. 'OK. I'll take you today.'

'Yes. Thanks mum!' Dan heard Maya dash out of the kitchen and get her games kit bag ready while Amy prepared to drive her to the match. When they were finally ready to leave they shouted a brief goodbye to Dan from downstairs and set off at speed down the drive. Soon they were out of sight.

All was quiet at last for Dan. Amy and her shrill, nagging voice had gone and the sun was rising over the trees outside the cottage. Dan loaded up his baggage into his car and set off on his own journey to the airport. His route took him across the Cotswold countryside. The sky was now a brilliant blue with white, puffy clouds sailing in procession above the hills and tree-tops.

Dan relaxed and turned on a classical music station on the radio, marvelling at the purity of the music: two violins and an orchestra spinning tunes together. The music touched his heart. The miles streamed past and he arrived at the airport in a good mood. He was looking forward to this trip and, for a moment, he forgot about his guilt and the fact that it was now more than a month since he'd spoken to his twin brother.

The queue for check-in was long but the plane took off on time. Flying was not Dan's favourite form of transport but, after take-off, the sound of clinking glass from an approaching drinks trolley helped him to relax.

'Something to drink, sir?' asked the hostess as she paused next to him.

'Whisky and ginger, please,' was the inevitable request from Dan. Old habits died hard.

The plane touched down at Frankfurt Airport on time. He stared at the passers-by as he made his way through the airport, and he couldn't help wondering what this visit had in store for him.

It was a short taxi ride to the hotel. Leichmatic had booked guests into the renowned and expensive Hotel Komforthaus which was also the venue for the company celebration that evening. He found that he had been booked into a suite with all sorts of luxuries. All very impressive, he thought as he sat down in the plush sitting room and opened the complimentary bottle of wine.

His phone rang. It was Amy.

'Dan, it's me. You said you'd text when you landed. You know how Maya gets worried when you travel.'

'Sorry, I was about to. Just checked in at the hotel and putting my feet up in my room.'

'I thought I'd let you know that Luke roused himself to collect our daughter after her match and drop her off at home. She's gone out with him for a walk now. I'm hoping he leaves after that because she's staying over at Laura's whilst I am out in Milchester tonight.'

'Oh, well that's something, I suppose,' he replied, irritated. 'Look, I don't like him either but she seems pretty smitten at the moment. She'll grow out of it. Perhaps when she heads to university. I can't see him doing a degree.'

'Listen,' Amy said, changing the subject. 'This meeting with your boss on Monday. Do you think they want to talk to you about a promotion. Maybe a move to the London office?'

'I don't know, Amy,' Dan replied. 'I really don't know yet. Look, I need to go now. Keep me posted on Maya. I'm very worried about her.'

'Yeah, OK. Whatever.' Amy hung up.

Dan opened his laptop, switched it on and scrolled through recent emails and other sales-related documents in the presentation pack he'd been sent. There was a promotional article translated from German, covering the history of Leichmatic's growth from a small plumbing firm in Frankfurt to a designer and manufacturer of kitchens that now operated in two countries.

He read the agenda for the day and then browsed through the guest list. There were a number of other UK sales managers but the majority were German. Dan recognised a few names of people he had recently dealt with in the Frankfurt offices, including Clara Meier, who regularly emailed and phoned him with sales information. He had always been cheered up by her young, chirpy and friendly German voice and her sometimes unusual English. He often wondered if she looked as attractive as she sounded on the phone.

After a while, his head kept nodding with the weight of sleepiness and the glass of wine he had already drunk. He made his way to the bed, set an alarm so he didn't oversleep and, before long, he had fallen back on the pillow and was fast asleep and snoring gently. It had been a long day so far and it wasn't over, as the company dinner was that evening.

Two hours later his alarm noisily alerted him that it was seven o'clock in the evening. He rapidly showered, dressed and took the lift down. Downstairs he joined the bar queue and came away with a glass of wine. He soon recognised a group of British colleagues who called him over to join them.

'Hi Dan, come and join us,' said Dave, the manager of the Manchester office. 'I think all us Brits will be sitting together in the dining room.'

Dan laughed. 'Thank God for that. I was wondering how I was going to survive. My German is not that good.'

After a while all UK guests were asked to move to the dining hall and given an allotted table for the dinner that was to follow. Everything was well-organised and a name card was placed at every seat. Dan found his place easily enough, but there was nobody sitting in the place on his right. He slyly picked up the card. It had a familiar name printed on it: Clara Meier.

Suddenly there was a hush in the room as the managing director and other senior management figures filed in towards the top table. Dan's attention was attracted by a young woman walking in with them. She looked typically German, tall with long blonde hair and blue eyes. She moved away from the management dignitaries and headed for his table. To Dan's surprise and delight, she made her way to the empty seat next to him. This was obviously Clara. She smiled at him and sat down, introducing herself.

'Good evening! I am Clara Meier.' She glanced at Dan's place name on the table and read it. 'Ah yes. You are Dan Barnes. We are talking on the telephone, aren't we? It is very good to be meeting with you now.'

'Yes, you're right,' replied Dan, loving her broken English. 'It's good to meet you, too, Clara.'

There was then a gradual silence as everyone sat down. Except the managing director, Hans Schmidt, who remained standing as he shuffled some papers. He tapped the microphone in front of him and gave a warm welcome to the UK guests before explaining that the evening was to celebrate twenty years of a company founded by his father.

Shortly afterwards the food was brought in and Dan was soon deep in conversation with Clara. They chatted about the company but also about themselves. Clara was in her early thirties and lived in Frankfurt. Dan explained that he lived in the English countryside and mentioned that he had a seventeen-year-old daughter. Clara joked that he must be very protective towards her and Dan responded, telling her that he certainly was. Dan was finding Clara very charming and, to his delight, she seemed to be responding to him in a similar way. The eye contact she was maintaining with him and the way she placed her hand on his sleeve when she was making a point all seemed to suggest the same thing. She was definitely taking a shine to him. As the meal drew to a close and guests started to leave, Clara was keen to continue their conversation.

'Would you like another drink, Dan? Shall we go to the bar?'

'Thanks, Clara. Good idea. But on one condition: the drinks will be on me.' He gave her a meaningful smile as they got up from their seats. The rest of the UK contingent melted away into the evening and Dan and Clara made their way to the bar.

'So what will you have?' he asked as they reached the bar.

'It's a gin and tonic for me,' she replied, looking straight into his eyes. 'Perhaps you can choose a gin for me?'

****

The rest of the evening passed by and the drinks helped Dan and Clara to relax further as they talked and laughed. Dan wondered whether she knew that he had a room here at the hotel. He eventually took the plunge.

'As you know, Clara, we're all staying in this hotel. But I'm not flying back tomorrow with the rest of the UK delegates. I am actually staying until Monday as I have a meeting with Herr Schneider at your offices.'

'OK, so that means you are free tomorrow? Did you have any plans?' asked Clara hopefully.

'I haven't made up my mind yet,' replied Dan. 'I don't really know Frankfurt so I have no idea what there is to see.'

'OK, you must see the Palmengarten,' Clara replied enthusiastically. 'In English this means a garden with palm trees. It is so beautiful at this time of year. There are so many spring flowers. I often love to go there myself.'

'Perhaps you could tell me how to get there?' asked Dan.

Clara looked directly at him.

'I am having an idea for us. I could come with you. Would you like me to take you to Palmengarten?'

'That would be good,' he replied, still wondering where the conversation was going. Was this beautiful woman just being friendly or did she feel the same attraction that he did.

'Maybe we could meet up here? How about that?' suggested Clara. 'In the reception area? At two o'clock? Oh yes, before I forget, let me give you my number. It will be good to be able to phone each other if we have any problems.'

'Great idea,' replied Dan. Phone numbers were exchanged. Clara briefly held his hands in hers.

'Until tomorrow,' she said, and then left him sitting at the bar, wondering if it had all been a dream.

****

The next day Dan woke up to the sound of bells ringing joyfully from Frankfurt's church towers. He thought about texting Maya to see if she was OK but he didn't want to seem like an overbearing father. He called Amy instead but there was no reply, which he thought odd. He tried the landline at the cottage. No reply there either. If Amy was not at home, where was she? What was she up to? And with whom?

Dan had recently become highly suspicious of the time she spent with those theatrical people. He had seen messages flash up on her phone from someone called Adam, and he wondered about the nature of their relationship. Something was definitely going on there. In the back of his mind though, he almost felt relief. The attraction he felt to Clara the night before was real. If Amy was already moving on, maybe he should, too. He texted Amy, suggesting he called her in the evening to check in on how Maya was doing.

After breakfast, Dan found a comfortable seat and a British Sunday paper in the reception area. There was not much news. There were the usual problems with the economy, a scandal involving a cabinet minister and another scandal related to the Royal Family. Dan put the paper down. It was predictable and boring. But he did not sit for long. He decided to take a walk through the city, see some sights and have lunch and a glass of wine before meeting with Clara back at the hotel in the afternoon.

Two'clock found Dan waiting anxiously in the hotel reception area. It was not long before a smart young woman dressed in jeans and jacket was approaching him, a wide smile on her face and her blonde hair tied up.

'Hello, Dan, how are you?'

Dan stood up, stroking his beard, rather lost for words. He had half expected her to cancel and find something else to do.

'Err... no, I am fine, thank you. And how about you?'

'I am fine, too,' replied Clara. 'It is good to be seeing you again.'

'So how do we get there?' asked Dan.

'We can walk to Palmengarten,' Clara smiled. 'Just come with me.'

On the street, she linked her arm with his and they walked off together, chatting away like old friends. Half an hour later they passed through the Palmengarten gates where they made their way around the flower beds which were overflowing with spring colours.

After a while, Clara suggested a rest, and so they stopped at a secluded bench and sat down together. It was a very quiet corner of the park and it was not long before Clara took the initiative and put a friendly hand on Dan's arm. Then she was leaning closer and closer. They were soon kissing. It had to happen.

Dan could still hardly believe it. A flash of Amy appeared in his mind but only for a second. Clara was beautiful and it had been a long time since someone had kissed him like this. He gave himself over to it. And, for a moment, he forgot about Amy and he forgot about the guilt he carried around with him now.

It was now late afternoon. The park would soon be closing its gates and Dan looked at his watch.

'So... Clara... what would you like to do now? Maybe come back to the hotel with me and have something to eat and then some drinks?'

He need not have asked. 'Yes' was already in her eyes and on her lips.

****

Later that evening, Dan and Clara were in the hotel restuarant, drinking red wine and digging into plates full of German meats. As the meal progressed, the effects of the wine became more and more evident and Clara clearly wanted to tell Dan about her past.

'I was married once but I live by myself now. My husband left me for someone else two years ago. He had been having other women for a long time that I didn't know about.'

'Oh no,' replied Dan. 'That must have been very difficult for you.'

'Yes it was...' Clara paused for a moment. 'But what about you, Dan? I know you have a daughter but what about a wife or a girlfriend? The women in the UK must be chasing you, right?'

'No, not at all,' replied Dan, which he meant in answer to her second question.

Clara smiled with relief and reached over the table and took his hands in hers, saying, 'You are a good man, Dan.' It was then that he realised that she had taken that as an answer to her first question. He briefly considered mentioning Amy – but Amy was not his wife. They hadn't even slept in the same bed for more than a year.

Eventually the food and the wine were finished. Dan, given courage by the alcohol, was very much hoping Clara might want to have another drink in his room.

'Would you... I mean to say – erm – you could come upstairs for a nightcap?' Clara smiled.

'Yes, of course' she said. 'I would love to.'

Dan put the meal on his room tab and they walked to the lifts together. When they reached the door to his room, Dan unlocked it with the key card and stood aside to let Clara in. She glanced around approvingly.

'They have put you in a nice place here,' she said. 'Perhaps we could order some room service. Maybe some more wine?'

Dan could think of nothing more that he wanted than the courage that another glass of wine would give him. He ordered another bottle for the room.

'Is there anything else you would like, Clara?

'Well, a nice shower would wake me up,' she said. 'It has been a very long day and I need to freshen up.'

'The shower is in there,' said Dan, pointing to the bathroom door. 'Please help yourself.' Clara soon disappeared and Dan could hear her happily singing away.

Shortly afterwards there was a knock on the bedroom door and the wine was delivered. Clara, who had heard what was going on, emerged from the shower and sat down on the edge of the bed. She was wearing a white fluffy dressing gown she had found in the bathroom. Dan poured her a glass and and passed it to her.

He was not really sure what to say, standing awkwardly next to the bed with his glass in his hand, so he said, 'Cheers, Clara.'

'Excuse me,' Clara was grinning. 'We say *prost* in Germany.'

'OK then. *Prost*,' said Dan, looking down at her sitting on the bed.

'So, why don't you come and sit down with me?' Clara suggested invitingly. She put down her glass on the bedside table, stood up and and opened up the dressing gown so that it was only loosely held together by the belt at the front. Underneath, she was completely naked.

'Come to me,' she whispered as she held out her arms. Dan hesitated for the briefest of moments. He had never cheated on Amy. He had always been faithful. Even when things started to get really bad. But he was lonely. And he knew their relationship was ending. He made a decision and walked towards Clara as she shook the gown off her shoulders onto the floor. She started to unbutton Dan's clothes, her hands moving all over him deliciously. They were soon on the bed, Clara riding him. He was in heaven. That night Clara took him to places he had never dreamt of.

****

On the following morning Clara woke up early and tugged at Dan's beard playfully.

'I loved last night.' said Clara.

'I did too. I'd like to see you again but I have to go into head office later this morning for an important meeting,' replied Dan regretfully.

Clara put her arms around him and gently pulled him closer.

'Don't worry, Dan. We will see each other again but I was thinking that perhaps… umm… as we have some time now and are still in bed, we could…'

Dan could not resist Clara's soft fingers.

It was some time later that Dan reluctantly slipped out of the bed and disappeared into the bathroom to take a shower. His phone, which he had left in the bedroom, began softly buzzing. Clara decided to take the call. It could be important. It could be his daughter.

'This is Dan's phone. Can I help you, please?' she asked politely.

'Who is this? Where's Dan? Is he there?' It was a woman's voice.

'Sorry,' replied Clara nervously. 'Who is this calling?'

'Amy.' Amy was getting very irritated by this response and started to question her.

'Amy?' Clara was confused. 'Are you Dan's daughter?'

'No, I'm the mother of his daughter. Anyway, who are you? And why do you have his phone? Where is he?'

'He is taking a shower,' replied Clara, who then suddenly realised her big mistake.

'Well, will you please ask him to call me back? And soon.' Amy slammed down the phone.

Dan emerged from the steamy shower with his towel around him and found Clara in tears.

'I am so sorry, Dan. Amy just phoned for you. And I thought it might be your daughter so I answered the phone. I am so stupid. You have a wife?'

'Clara,' Dan said. 'You're not stupid. I should have been honest with you. I still live with Maya's mother but our relationship – it's everything but over. We don't sleep together. We've only stayed together for the sake of our daughter. But I should have told you… I should have been honest.'

Clara looked up at him, wondering if he was being honest with her now. She slowly stood up and faced him.

'I know one thing, Dan,' she said. 'I have loved to talk to you and having you close to me. It has all been like a dream. But now you will have to go home to Amy and finish things. I am so sorry as I like you so very much. But this always seems to be the way for me. Another sad goodbye.'

She rapidly dressed, collected her belongings and was all set to go. She gave him a long, deep goodbye kiss and then opened the room door. She turned, smiling at him.

'But I will speak to you over the phone again soon?' Dan ventured. They had spoken so often before and he didn't want any awkwardness when they worked together again.

Clara shook her head sadly. 'Unfortunately, no. I was promoted to the director of the wider Berlin area the day before the celebration. I will no longer be overseeing the UK business. *Auf weidersehen*, Dan. Maybe one day we really will meet again. Maybe when you become free?'

Clara closed the door behind her as she left. Another chapter in Dan's chequered life had ended. He sat down on the bed which was still imbued with Clara's sweet scent. She was such a lovely woman. But she was also right. He now knew he must take a decision that would change his relationship with Amy in a very real way. Perhaps they were both ready to finally end it.

****

After breakfast, Dan finished his packing, checked out of the hotel and walked slowly to the Leichmatic offices where he had his meeting to attend before catching the flight home. The prospect of the meeting had raised a wide range of issues for Dan to think about. What was his future with Leichmatic? He hoped he was up for promotion. Maybe a senior position in the London area? That could be the break he needed.

At precisely two o'clock Dan was shown into the director's office. Helmut Schneider, a rotund and rather pompous man, greeted Dan and asked him to sit down. He proceeded to bombard Dan with polite chat.

'You have had a good time here in Frankfurt?'

'Yes, very good, thank you.'

'Would you like a coffee?'

'No, thank you. I am fine.'

'Isn't it warm for the time of year?'

'Yes, it is rather warm.'

The meeting then took on a more serious turn. Schneider coughed nervously and cleared his throat.

'Mr Barnes, are you happy in your present post in the UK?'

'Yes, very much so, but it would be good to progress to a more challenging sales region – London and the south east, for example.'

Schneider continued, 'So, you feel that you are not fully satisfied in your present post?'

'On the contrary, I am fully satisfied with my job. But I do like a change and a challenge from time to time. So if there were maybe openings in other, more prominent branches—'

'You see, this is the situation,' Schneider interupted. He rustled through his papers, cleared his throat again and stared out of the window. He looked decidedly uncomfortable. 'I don't know whether or not you know, but UK sales have been disappointing in the last three years. The rest of the business is thriving but there seems to be something missing in the UK market. We have been talking of a merger with Kuchenjager. But they are reluctant to get around the table until we cut some of the dead wood.'

'Dead wood?' repeated Dan, looking worried.

'I need you to know that we are looking seriously at cutting some of the smaller regional offices and consolidating our UK presence.'

Dan replied, very concerned about Schneider's attitude, 'Surely our sales aren't that bad? We made a good profit last year and my team have been working really hard at finding new business. We've just had that amazing celebration of the company on Saturday. How can you possibly be thinking about cutting our branches.'

Schneider paused, tapping his pen on his desk.

'It's just business, Mr Barnes,' he said, calmly. 'We need to make sure we're making efficiencies and keeping the company successful.'

Dan gave a sigh. Was he going to lose his job?

'Please do not despair, Mr Barnes – may I call you Daniel?' Schneider said. 'Nothing is certain. I just wanted to let you know that we will be sending people from the office here to assess the performance your branch. They will also be assessing several other branches. Yours is not the only one under consideration.'

'I see. Thank you, Herr Schneider. I will bear all this mind.'

It was a very worried Dan that left the Leichmatic offices for the airport. He caught his early evening flight home to the UK. As his plane gained altitude, he watched Frankfurt disappear underneath him, and thought of Clara who was already many miles away. The night before already felt very distant.

Dan knew that he would face an angry Amy when he got back to Birch Cottage. But he was also sure that Amy was having an affair herself. Their relationship was over, wasn't it? Dan could now see the beginning of an end for both of them. He had been preparing himself for it for years but now it was here, and he suddenly felt sad. Would he and Amy be able to separate with minimum damage to Maya's world? Maybe Maya would side with Amy? That didn't bear thinking about.

Dan needed refreshment. He could hear the drinks trolley rattling down the aisle of the plane. He scanned through the menu. He needed a stiff drink to be fully prepared for the conflict waiting for him at home.

Possibly a whisky and ginger.

Chapter 8

A month had slipped by since Dan's encounter with Clara in Frankfurt. Much to Dan's surprise, Amy never confronted him about why his phone call was answered by another woman. He had been prepared for a showdown, some sort of blazing argument where they would finally end things. Instead, Amy had stressed that they both needed to focus on Maya and her exams. Once she was at university, Amy said, they would talk about things. Amy's calm had disarmed Dan and he found himself unable to act. But, in the coming weeks, their relationship had gone from bad to worse. Amy was often out with the players until late and she and Dan barely spent any time together. When they did, they were tetchy with each other. But they knew that whilst Maya was still living with them home life had to remain as normal as possible.

Despite her parents' best efforts, Maya knew something was wrong and she recognised that her parents were at daggers drawn – they were always arguing, shouting, slamming doors and then retreating, each to their own room. She also knew that it was her very close friendships with her college mates that really kept her sane.

And so it was that on a warm early summer evening Maya and her best college mate, Laura, were sitting at a table outside the Café Italia in Milchester, putting the world to rights. They had just taken a gruelling exam that day and couldn't wait for it all to end. Laura, with her dyed blonde hair and ample proportions, was a loud and ditzy girl, and a loyal friend of Maya.

'Guess what? I have a great idea for how to celebrate the end of exams,' Laura exclaimed. She paused, a grin spreading across her face, waiting for Maya's reaction.

'OK then. Spit it out,' replied Maya who was familiar with Laura's 'great ideas' which were usually outlandish.

'Now listen to this, Maya. My parents are going away on holiday to Barbados in a week's time and so I'll be home alone. And… our house will be available and ideal for a party to celebrate the end of the exams.'

The more practical Maya was not so sure this was a good idea. Laura's parents were very well off, their house was large, grand and set in a woodland park with a lake. Maya sensed disaster in Laura's party plan which would invite a bunch of rowdy teenagers into that environment. She couldn't help but be intrigued by the idea of a party, though.

'Bloody hell, Laura, wouldn't they disown you if they found out?'

'Probably. But,' replied Laura, 'would they ever have to know? We would obviously have to be really careful. We wouldn't want the house getting trashed.' Laura seemed so very excited about the idea but Maya was secretly very worried about what could happen to the house – and would Luke come?

Laura continued, 'Nick knows someone who will be able to organise all the music. Nick is really cool, helpful and very good with his hands. I can't wait for you to meet him.' She paused, grinning at Maya. Nick was Laura's new boyfriend and Maya knew exactly what she meant about Nick's hands.

'OK, maybe it would be fun,' Maya said, glancing at her watch. 'Oh my God. Is that the time? My mum is picking me up. I really gotta go now, babe. So sorry.'

She rushed off, leaving a five-pound note on the table for Laura to pay for their coffees.

Later that evening, Laura and Maya had a long phone conversation to discuss the party in detail, including who should be on the guestlist. It would be on a Saturday at the end of their exams.

****

And so, after the final exam had finished, at long last it was the day of the party. Maya spent ages in her bedroom trying on various dresses and looking at herself in her full-length mirror. How did she look? Her girlfriends at college had told her that they would die for her slim build, raven-dark hair, and dark brown eyes.

Maya turned away from the mirror and had an urge to make an entry in her diary – a very secret book that she had started writing when she was fourteen and had become seriously interested in boys. She kept the diary at the back of her dressing table drawer in a cardboard box meant for her copy of the Holy Bible. She had removed and carefully hidden away the original volume in her wardrobe. Maya retrieved her diary and flicked through the pages, muttering to herself as she worked her way through the successes and failures of her love life so far.

'First boyfriend: Max… Hmmm. A bit of a dweeb. Didn't last long. Oh my God, was that really four years ago?'

When she reached the section devoted to Mark, who had been her first serious boyfriend when she was sixteen, she stopped turning the pages. Her relationship with him had been intense and she had been heartbroken when his family decided to emigrate to the States.

'Oh yes. He was the real thing for sure… mmm… oh yes.'

Maya then turned to her recent entries about Luke. They had now been an item for six months. He had the good looks of an Adonis. Maya loved his fair hair and blue eyes and athletic body. She began a new entry in the diary.

> 'Exams finished at long last. Thank God. Getting ready for party tonight. Really looking forward to seeing Luke again.'

Maya closed the diary and carefully hid it in the box inside the dressing table drawer. She looked at her watch. She was running late and needed to get to Laura's house by six o'clock to help her set up the party. Her mum had promised to give her a lift.

'Come on, Maya. We need to go. Now! And I mean now!' She heard her mother shout up the stairs.

Downstairs, Amy was getting exasperated. She needed to get to Milchester, after dropping Maya off, for a rehearsal of Shakespeare's *As You Like It* where she would also see Adam Ashworth again. In desperation she shouted up to Maya's bedroom again.

Maya eventually appeared, looking flustered and they bundled into the car. They were soon flying down the drive and along the road to Laura's house. Maya was very apologetic.

'Sorry, Mum. I just needed to get everything ready for the party. I'm going to stay over though so you won't have to come and pick me up until tomorrow.'

'And I presume Luke will also be going,' enquired Amy.

Maya hesitated. 'Yes, I guess so.'

'And is he staying over too?' Amy asked pointedly.

'I've no idea, actually. Honestly though, Mum. I'm not ready for anything like that with Luke. You don't have to worry.'

'OK,' Amy sounded relieved. 'And it's not you that I don't trust, it's him.'

There then followed an awkward silence between them. At long last the car drew up to the front of Laura's country house and they were met at the door by her and Nick – Laura's new boyfriend. Laura was bursting with excitement.

'You do look fab, Maya. Stunning, in fact,' said Laura enviously as they passed through the house to the garden terrace where it appeared that Nick's friend had just finished setting up the speakers.

'Nick, this is Maya, my bestest friend in the whole world,' said Laura. Nick smiled at Maya.

Maya and Nick helped Laura set out some food on a buffet table as a well as beers and bottles of wine in ice buckets. By seven o'clock the other guests had started to arrive. Nick's friend started the music and the partygoers milled about on the terrace where they had a view of the gardens, the lake and a summer house. The weather was perfect – the sun was starting to sink down towards the trees and was reflected in the lake below.

As the evening wore on, a heavier rhythm of dance music started up. The air outside was still and warm. Everyone was soon dancing on the terrace. Everyone except Maya. Luke had not yet put in an appearance. She had been waiting for him to arrive all evening.

'Where the hell is Luke? What is he playing at?' she asked Laura as they stood at the side of the terrace and watched the dancing.

'I'm sure he'll be here soon,' Laura said.

'I need more wine, Laura.'

'Help yourself but do go easy, please.'

Maya headed for the drinks table and took a big swig from an already opened wine bottle. She gulped down yet another swig and received a disapproving glare from Laura. She put the bottle down and left to join the dancers.

'Are you OK?' shouted Laura anxiously over the noise. She could see that Maya had been knocking back a lot of wine.

'Sure... I'm fine. Just letting off some steam,' replied Maya, looking anxiously around her. 'Where the fuck is that Luke?'

Shortly afterwards, a dishevelled Luke arrived at the party. He caught sight of Maya dancing on her own and immediately moved over to her, weaving his way through the other dancers.

'Found me in the end, did you?' asked Maya sarcastically.

'Sorry, sorry. I had some stuff I needed to sort out. I will tell you later. Come on.'

The couple walked away together from the dance floor.

'Did you bring anything for the drinks table?' asked Maya, who was beginning to feel less angry now that Luke had arrived.

'I brought your favourite vodka, babe. Smirnoff.' He produced the bottle from behind his back and grinned.

'Mmmm, vodka,' replied Maya. She thought that her boyfriend did look rather fetching in his tight jeans. She slid into his arms and kissed him.

Luke looked relieved and whispered in Maya's ear, 'Why don't we chill out by the lake for a while?'

Luke could be very persuasive and Maya melted. They collected a couple of glasses and made their way down the garden to the lakeside summer house, away from the other teenage partygoers. They sat down and Luke pulled her closer and they shared a long kiss. Then he poured a vodka. Then another – was it two? Or was it three? Luke kept refilling her glass. Luke was clearly feeling very amorous and Maya was feeling very drunk. She remembered what she had told her mother. She *wasn't* ready for that with Luke.

'Let's go back to the house, I want to have a dance,' she suggested in a slurred voice as she struggled to stand up.

'Sure,' replied Luke, sounding disappointed. He helped her to her feet.

The music was still thumping its heavy rhythms as the couple slowly walked back up the path up to the terrace. Maya needed the support of Luke's arm as she walked unsteadily towards the lights of the house. She staggered onto the dance floor and found Laura, who was dancing with Nick. Luke stood looking surly at the side of the dance floor as his girlfriend swayed to the music looking unsteady on her feet.

'Oh my God, Maya. You are so drunk. What did Luke give you?' asked Laura .

'I drank some vodka,' Maya slurred. 'You know what, I'm not feeling so good. I feel so hot and dizzy.' Maya was feeling more and more unstable and her head was swimming.

Suddenly Maya's eyes fluttered and instinctively, Nick and Laura reached out to hold her as she collapsed. They immediately fell to their knees as they guided her gently to the ground where they lay her on her back. Maya moaned, sounding sick. The dancers around her formed a circle and at the side of the dancefloor, Luke looked panicked. He then turned and ran rapidly through the house and out of the front door. The music was abruptly turned off. Most looked on helplessly as Nick and another friend carefully lifted Maya from the floor and made her comfortable on a nearby wooden bench with some cushions. She wasn't unconscious but she didn't look well at all.

'Where the hell is Luke?' Laura asked angrily, looking around for him. 'He was here a second ago. How much has she had to drink? Has she taken anything else?'

Luke seemed to have evaporated. Nobody knew where he had gone. They had all been focused on Maya's collapse and the need to help her. Laura was now extremely concerned. Had Luke spiked Maya's drink with something else?

Maya very slowly came around.

'Maya,' Laura said. 'Did Luke give you anything else other than vodka?'

'No...' Maya said, groggily, 'I don't think so. I just had too much vodka. I don't feel well, Laura. I want to go home.'

Laura asked Nick to get the music going again and went into the house to phone Maya's parents. Dan picked up the call, sounding very grumpy.

'Hello? Maya? What's going on?'

'It's Laura, Mr Barnes. I'm so sorry,' said Laura in an apologetic voice. 'But I am afraid Maya is not at all well. She has had a little too much to drink and she just wants to get home. Can you come and pick her up?'

'Yes, of course. We'll be with you soon. I just hope she is OK.' Dan was grateful that he had only had one glass of wine himself. He sent a quick text to Amy at rehearsals to let her know he was collecting Maya. She messaged back almost immediately to say she was on her way back from Milchester.

Dan dressed rapidly, and was soon on the road.

Laura waited anxiously near her front door. After what seemed an eternity Dan arrived and Laura showed him into the house. He started bombarding her with questions as they hurried their way through the house to the terrace.

'Is she alright?'

'Yes,' replied Laura. 'She is OK, really. I think

maybe she has just had a few too many.'

'Is Luke here?'

Laura was caught off guard by this question.

'He was here but I think he left. I've no idea where. She says that he gave her some vodka but she'd already had a lot of wine before he arrived.'

By now they had reached the edge of the terrace where Maya was being looked after by another college friend. Maya was now sitting up and sipping at a glass of water.

'Maya,' Dan crouched down in front of her. 'Are you OK?'

'Mmhmm,' Maya nodded, sadly. 'But I feel a bit sick.'

'Hmmm. Too much to drink?' muttered Dan.

'I'm sorry, Dad,' Maya said miserably as Laura helped her to her feet. Dan put his arm around his daughter.

'Did her head hit the ground when she fell?' Dan asked, wondering whether he needed to get Maya to a hospital.

'No, Mr Barnes,' Laura said. 'Nick and I managed to catch her. But she has been sick.' Maya groaned in agreement.

'Let's get you home where you can sleep this off, my love,' Dan said gently. They walked slowly towards his car.

Just as they set off Dan called out to Laura through the car window.

'If you see that creep Luke, tell him I will be having words with him.'

****

The following day, Maya woke up with a hangover from hell. She came slowly downstairs and found her parents sitting at the kitchen table drinking coffee.

'Feeling better?' Amy asked.

'Not really,' Maya said. 'Oh, I'm so sorry. I've let you both down.'

'It's not us you've let down,' Dan said, softly, 'it's yourself. You need to take better care of yourself, Maya.'

'Was it Luke who gave you all that vodka?' Amy asked. 'And did he give you anything else?'

'He seemed to disappear pretty quickly when you were sick,' Dan said. 'Laura said that he left very rapidly. Huh! Some boyfriend he is.'

'Look,' Amy said, seriously. 'You're going to be at university this autumn. And we won't be there to pick you up. You need to make sure you know your limits and don't get yourself into these situations. It's not safe, Maya.'

'I know,' Maya said. 'Believe me, I have learned my lesson.'

'And Luke?' Dan asked.

'I'm sure he had a good reason for not staying, Dad,' she said, sheepishly. 'I just want to give him a chance to explain.'

Maya shuffled sadly upstairs to shower.

'I hope she has learned a lesson,' Dan said. 'I was really scared last night when I got that call. And I'll kill that Luke when I see him again.'

'That won't help anything,' Amy said. 'She's going to have to learn herself what he's like. US being against him just makes him more attractive. When she's at university she'll see that she can do so much better. And he'll be far away from her.'

They fell into silence. Both of them were considering the changes that might come for all of them when Maya was finally at university.

After showering, Maya called her friend to apologise for ruining the party.

'I am so sorry, Laura. I really don't know what happened. One minute I was dancing the night away and the next thing I remember, I was lying on the floor, feeling bad. Did I throw up?'

'Oh yes. And your dad looked pretty worried,' Laura paused for a moment. 'You don't have to answer this, but are you sure that Luke didn't tempt you with anything stronger than alcohol? Did he maybe slip something into your glass?'

'I really don't think so, Laura. I know Luke is sometimes crazy but he wouldn't do that to me,' replied Maya.

'He certainly didn't stick around to help when you were sick,' Laura said ruefully.

'Yeah, I know,' Maya said. 'I'd like to give him the chance to explain what happened though. I've tried to call him this morning but he's not picking up. If you see him, can you tell him to call me?'

'Sure,' Laura said.

'I feel really rough,' Maya said. 'I'd better go.'

The call ended and Maya made her unsteady way to the bathroom.

Chapter 9

Two long weeks had passed since Maya's episode at the party. Maya had tried messaging the elusive Luke numerous times, but there had been no reply. She had tried phoning him. There was still no reply. Then, suddenly, when she was just about to give up, she got a message from him out of the blue.

> 'Babe, I'm sorry I had to go at the party. I got a call and had to go. When I looked for you, I couldn't find you. Now I know that's because you were being looked after. If I'd have known that you were sick, I would never have left. You know I love you. How about tonight in Milchester for drinks? Let me know where and what time.'

Maya was doubtful. Laura had said that Luke had watched as she collapsed and left after that. But maybe Laura was wrong. Maybe Luke *had* been called away by something important. She messaged him back and invited him to come to a favourite pub, the Riverside in Milchester where she was meeting Laura and some others later.

Amy was in an exceptionally bad mood at home

that day. She had just been involved in a furious argument with Dan about how his drinking wasn't setting a good example for their daughter. When Maya told her she was meeting Luke that evening, her mood worsened. Even so she still agreed to drop Maya off in Milchester to see her friends. As she and Maya set off in the car, Amy was at boiling point. Her anger was directed at Luke and she made her feelings about him very clear.

'I really don't know what you see in that Luke,' she exclaimed. 'I really don't. He always seems to be bad news. How on earth can you trust him after what happened at that party?'

'But, Mum, he says that he didn't know I was sick,' replied Maya. 'He has had his bad times, I know that. But I am really sure I can put him right.'

Amy was furious and put her foot on the accelerator. Maya rammed her earphones into her ears to shut out any more comments from her mother.

Half an hour later, as they reached the outskirts of Milchester, Maya had begun to forget Amy's harsh words. It was a warm, calm July evening and she reckoned it was going to be a good evening out. By the time her mother dropped her off at the Riverside pub in Milchester, the cold atmosphere between them had warmed a little.

'Have a good time, Maya,' her mother said as she pulled up. 'But please don't drink too much tonight and do be careful.'

'Thanks, Mum. Nick is going to give me a lift home.'

As Amy drove off, Maya felt happy that they had parted on better terms. She soon met up with Laura and Nick. They all sat down at a table overlooking the River Avon. Luke was late.

'So where is Luke?' asked Laura pointedly. She wasn't as ready to believe and forgive Luke as her friend.

'I'll give him a call. I bet he is nearby somewhere,' said Maya. She was right, Luke was outside and soon joined them out in the pub garden.

The drinks now flowed freely for most of the others but Maya made sure that she stuck with soft drinks that night. The queues at the bar grew longer and the noise level louder. Luke was on good form, cracking jokes and trying to flirt with Laura – much to Maya's irritation.

It was late. The pub had called last orders. The sun had finally sunk and it was getting darker.

'I don't want to head home just yet,' Laura announced. 'Where can we go and hang out for a while longer?'

'Hey, guys. I know a really cool place,' Luke chipped in. 'It's just a short walk down by the river near the bridge. I think there are seats and a table there.'

Nick, who knew the area well, looked very dubious about Luke's geography and the mention of a table and seats. As far as he knew there were no tables or seats in that direction, just a rough pathway that led along the river. But he kept quiet. He didn't want to start an argument. The group walked down the grassy slope until they got to the river. Here the path became increasingly treacherous because of tree roots crossing over the pathway. The river rushed past on one side of them.

'Watch where you are treading!' warned Luke as they stumbled their way down the slope. The path was narrowing and they had to walk in single file, as the light faded fast over the river's rapidly flowing and darkening water. Maya was having trouble seeing her way in the dark and she occasionally stumbled on the path. She was horribly aware of being so close to the dark swirling water of the river. It brought her back to that day some months ago when Sophie had fallen into the waters and drowned. She started to feel very scared and wished that Luke was holding her hand. But he was charging ahead, leading their group.

'Not far now,' promised Luke cheerily, although he was secretly having doubts about there being seats by the path. Had he got it wrong? Was he thinking of somewhere else? But he said nothing.

Suddenly the quiet evening was shattered by an ear-piercing scream. Maya had tripped over a tree root and had been sent tumbling down the river bank. She tried to stop herself but she fell straight into the water, crying out for help and kicking wildly as the rapid currents tried to pull her downstream.

Laura and Nick looked at Luke as if to say, 'Come on now and do something.' But Luke was transfixed by what he had seen and did not seem to be able to move.

'Come on! Somebody!' shouted Laura, 'We've got to get Maya out of there. She's panicking.'

It was true. They could see Maya splashing and thrashing, trying to keep her head above the water, but then disappearing again and coming back up, gasping for breath as the river pulled on her.

It was Nick who saved the day. With no further thought, he kicked off his shoes and lowered himself into the river where he swam out to Maya in the dark, swirling water. He caught hold of her and brought her back to the riverbank.

'Thank goodness that you were with us, Nick, and kept off the booze,' exclaimed Laura as she and Luke helped the bedraggled Maya to safety up the river bank and Nick pulled himself up over the bank. Luke said nothing. He seemed to be in a daze.

Maya sat down, hunched up on the narrow riverbank path, her arms around her knees. She was exhausted, traumatised, dripping wet, shaking with the cold and muttering to herself. Her speech was mostly unintelligible, but occasionally words such as 'Sophie' and 'dark water' could be made out.

Laura was extremely concerned about her friend. She was shaken and soaking wet. And now her boyfriend was also wet and cold. They needed to get dry and warm.

'We need to get Maya home,' she said, firmly. 'Help me get her back to your car up at the pub, Nick. And you've got to get dry, too.'

Nick gently helped the shivering Maya to her feet and began to take her back to the car. Laura looked relieved. Her new man was really showing his true colours. Luke, however, remained quiet. Laura shoved past him. It had been a stupid suggestion to come this close to the river in the dark and he hadn't even lifted a finger to help when his girlfriend was in trouble. He was again showing how useless he was.

They passed by the pub and made their way to the car. Thankfully Maya was now becoming more secure on her feet and more coherent in her speech. Nick produced a blanket from the boot and draped it around Maya's shoulder. He took off his wet jumper and put on a dry one that he had on the back seat. They were all soon in Nick's car, heading for Birch Cottage. Maya sat in the back seat with Luke who had still said absolutely nothing.

It was the early hours by the time the car reached its destination. Dan had stayed up, anxious that Maya got home safely. He had just started to get worried about the late hour when he heard the arrival of the car and opened the front door to be met by a very damp Maya together with Laura and Nick. An embarrassed-looking Luke was standing behind them. Dan had not bargained on seeing Luke that night. He was invariably bad news.

'What the hell happened?' Dan asked, sweeping Maya into his arms.

'Maya slipped and fell into the river,' Laura explained.

'My God,' Dan said, holding Maya at arm's length to look at her. 'Are you OK, Maya?'

'I am,' Maya said. 'Just wet. And cold.'

'What the hell were you all doing so close to the river in the dark?' Dan asked. He noted that Luke stared straight at the ground and frowned.

'It was just an accident, Dad,' Maya said.

'Nick jumped in and saved her,' Laura said, pointedly. 'He's tonight's hero.' Nick looked embarrassed.

Maya continued, sounding less and less sure of herself, 'It really wasn't anyone's fault. I should have looked where I was going.'

Dan looked over his daughter's head at her useless boyfriend and scowled. Why did his daughter always seem to get in trouble when this boy was around? Luke continued to look at the ground. Dan sighed. He needed to make sure that Maya was OK.

'Amy!' shouted Dan up the stairway. 'Wake up. Come and give us a hand, will you. We have a problem here.'

Amy soon appeared, bustling down the stairs in a bright pink dressing gown.

'Oh my God, Maya. What have you done? What happened to you?'

'Maya's had an accident. She slipped and fell into the river,' Laura explained.

'Oh no!' exclaimed Amy. She glanced at Dan and they both knew they were thinking of the day Sophie drowned. What if something had happened to Maya? It didn't bear thinking about.

'Nick saved her,' Laura repeated again.

'You look suspiciously dry, Luke,' Amy said. 'Did you not want to get your clothes wet?'

'I... I would have gone in, of course,' he stammered. 'But Nick was already in the water and so I helped to pull Maya out.'

'I don't remember that,' Laura said, sharply. 'As far as I remember you just stood there.'

'Oh really?' said Dan. He turned to Amy. 'Anyway, enough of this. Amy, you'd better get our girl into a hot bath before she gets pneumonia. Look, her teeth are chattering. Where are the towels? And you, Nick, you need to dry out too.'

Amy took Maya upstairs and wrapped her up in towels and ran her a hot steaming bath.

'Mum,' Maya said, sheepishly. 'Can Luke stay tonight in the other spare room? It honestly wasn't his fault. It was a stupid accident and I'm really OK.' As soon as Maya was sitting in the bath Amy came back down the stairs. She had a number of thoughts as she watched Nick finish drying his damp hair with a towel. Should she let Luke stay? He could go back with Nick? But she wanted to trust Maya who had already had quite an upsetting night. Without talking to Dan, she took Luke aside and made a suggestion.

'You can stay here tonight, Luke. We have a spare room.'

Luke nodded his head. 'Yeah, thanks. That would be great.'

'Dan,' she called through to him in the kitchen, 'can you show Luke our spare bedroom? He can stay here for one night.'

'What?' exclaimed Dan, surprised and annoyed. 'Hang on, who said *he* could stay over?'

'I did, of course,' replied Amy. 'It's just one night and we all need to get some rest after this. We can talk more in the morning.'

'You're going to let him stay here, in our house, after all this?' replied Dan, who was getting highly irate with the situation and particularly with Amy. But she had made up her mind. Nick and Laura said their goodbyes and drove off into the dark night. Dan muttered expletives under his breath as Amy returned upstairs to help Maya get out of the bath. He then, reluctantly and grumpily, took Luke upstairs and showed him the spare room.

The cottage finally settled down for a fitful sleep. It

was a very disturbed night. Dan found himself wracked by familiar nightmares – only this time the figure drowning in the water wasn't Sophie, it was Maya.

The next morning, Dan was up early and down in the kitchen, preparing coffee when he heard movement from the spare bedroom. Luke must be making his way to the bathroom. He wanted to have a word with him to find out what had really happened by the riverside the previous evening and why Luke hadn't been the one to jump in after his girlfriend.

Dan crept upstairs and entered the spare room. Luke was clearly still in the bathroom. He noticed that Luke had left his mobile phone by the side of the bed. Dan could not resist having a look at it. A message was on the screen:

> 'Thanks for the lovely time we had together on Friday night. Can't wait until our next meeting. Sarah xx.'

Dan was furious. Luke was two-timing his daughter. He needed to have some serious words. He then caught sight of Luke's jeans on a stool in the corner. He saw a small plastic bag filled with white powder poking out of one of the jeans pockets. He pulled it out and looked at it. Was this what he thought it was? He quickly hid it in his own pocket, together with the phone. He was incensed. Had Luke brought drugs into his daughter's life and his own home?

Dan again heard Luke moving around and opening the bathroom door. Dan moved swiftly out of the spare room onto the landing and stood at the top of the stairs to confront Luke. He needed to find out the truth. He showed Luke the packet of powder.

'I found this in your jeans, Luke.'

'That belongs to a friend,' Luke said. 'I am not into that sort of thing.'

Dan could not stomach Luke's constant lying. He put the drugs back into his pocket, then pulled out the mobile phone and held it in front of him.

'What about this, then?'

'Yeah, that's my phone,' replied Luke. He made a move to take it. But Dan held it firmly in his hand.

'Who is Sarah? Are you seeing another girl behind my daughter's back? Come on now, Luke. I've seen the message on your phone. Tell me the truth.'

This time it was Luke who was angry and he, again, tried to snatch the phone from Dan but failed.

At the sound of the commotion, Amy and Maya rushed out of their rooms and found Dan and Luke sizing up to each other. Maya screamed for the two combatants to stop.

'Your bloody husband had no right to touch my property,' Luke shouted at Amy. He launched himself at Dan and snatched the phone back.

'He's a liar,' Dan said to his daughter. 'I've just seen a message from a girl called Sarah on his phone. Are you seeing other girls, Luke?'

'Luke…?' Maya looked at him.

Luke laughed, before spluttering, 'She's my sister.'

'You've never mentioned you had a sister,' Maya murmured.

Dan sneered, 'You expect me to believe all that crap? You are a loser, Luke. Just get out of my house and keep your hands off my daughter. Just get out! Now!'

Luke shouted back at him, 'I'll get my own back. Just you wait and see how wrong you are, you crazy bastard.'

He pushed past Dan and into the spare room. He returned, seconds later, wearing his jeans. He rushed down the stairs and out into the garden, stumbling as he went. The three of them followed him down and could see him from the kitchen window as he made his way down the drive, clutching his phone to his ear and speaking to someone.

'Probably scrounging a lift from one of his mates,' muttered Dan to Amy. She was comforting Maya, who was sobbing, totally dumbfounded by the outbreak of violence and wondering if all that her dad had said was in fact actually true. Was Luke cheating on her? He'd never mentioned a sister called Sarah. She could only come to one conclusion. Nothing about Luke added up anymore.

****

All was quiet at Birch Cottage later that Sunday afternoon. Dan went for a woodland walk. It was a hot, humid summer's day and the trees spread a cooling green canopy over the footpath. He thought over the events of the last twenty-four hours as he strode along. He knew that he had lost his temper with Luke, but he had not been able to see any other way of reacting to the situation. One thing that had really annoyed him was Amy's soft treatment of Luke the night before. It had been Amy that had invited him to stay overnight and that made him boil with rage.

While Dan was away from the cottage and having these deep thoughts, Amy was left in the cottage with Maya. The two of them sat outside in the garden on their favourite wooden bench as the afternoon sun dropped lower in the sky. They talked and talked – trying to put everything that had happened into perspective. They were still there when Dan returned from his walk.

'What have you decided to do about Luke?' he asked.

Amy sighed and answered before Maya could. 'She's still not convinced about this other girl.'

'Well,' Dan said, slowly. 'Maybe this will convince you.' Dan produced the bag of powder that he had found in Luke's pocket. 'Did you know about this? I found it in Luke's jeans.'

'What is it?' Maya said.

'It looks to me like drugs,' Dan said. Maya went pale.

'No way!' Maya responded angrily.

'You've got to finish with him, my love,' Amy said, softly. 'He's no good for you. You deserve much better than him. And it won't be long until you're at university. It'll be a whole new start for you.'

Maya looked defeated and nodded but she still felt like crying. She couldn't keep making excuses for Luke. She slowly made her way up to her bedroom, knowing that she needed to make a decision. She sent Luke a text message:

> 'I can't do this anymore. It's too difficult. I need some time apart to get my head straight.'

Luke texted back straightaway, briefly and to the point:

> 'Whatever, bitch.'

Maya felt the shock of his hurtful response but she knew, in that moment, she had made the right decision. Later, a tearful Maya broke the news of the break-up to her parents, who hugged and comforted their sobbing daughter.

For Dan and Amy words were not necessary. They both knew that, despite all the tears and drama, they were overwhelmingly relieved that Maya had seen Luke for what he really was. Both Maya's heart and her body would be safer without Luke's influence.

And for Maya there was another milestone looming. In a matter of weeks, she would get her exam results which would largely dictate her future. Despite their efforts to keep their troubles hidden from Maya, their dying relationship had inevitably become very obvious to their daughter. Life at the cottage was becoming a battlefield. Maya wondered what would happen when she left the nest. Armageddon maybe? She secretly hoped that her parents would either come to terms with each other or that one of them would make the decision to leave.

She knew from watching her mother's recent comings and goings that she was certainly in close contact with someone else – possibly in her local drama group. Maya guessed that it would most likely be her mother who would go and build a new life elsewhere. And, if that were to happen, it would mean her father would be completely on his own in their lonely cottage with all its memories. Maya was getting very upset about the whole situation at home. But what could she do?

Chapter 10

The night before Maya was due to receive her exam results, she could not sleep. She was in her room, lying awake in bed at midnight, angry, tired and anxious. She was still hurting from Luke's crude response to their break-up. She was also worried about the results she would get the next day. And to add to all this she was also concerned by her parents' rocky relationship. She had no idea what might happen to them when she eventually left home for a new life at University of London where she would carry on with her studies in English Literature.

She propped herself up in bed and flicked on her bedside lamp. She stared at the walls of her familiar and cosy bedroom – full of photos of family, friends and happy events. She wondered what pictures would be there in a year's time. But then she caught sight of something moving on the ceiling in the corner of the room. A spider was busy spinning its web. Was it an omen? Maya shuddered, switched off the light and burrowed under the bedclothes. Thoughts and images of her home and her friends were flashing through her mind. But eventually she managed to get to sleep, totally exhausted.

****

The next day, Maya's alarm woke her with a jolt. She hated the insistent sound of that alarm. Results day had at last dawned: exam grades would be released and Maya and her fellow students would converge on Milchester College to collect them.

Maya got up and looked closely at herself in her bedroom mirror. All her hard work for the exams and the events of the last few weeks had taken their toll. Dark shadows were under her brown eyes, her skin was pallid and her hair was tousled and tangled. What a wreck, she thought.

She looked at her phone. It was six thirty. She must get moving. The results would be ready at eight. She could hear her mother downstairs preparing breakfast. But when Maya eventually arrived in the kitchen, she could not stomach the idea of bacon and eggs.

'Sorry, Mum, I really don't think I can eat anything. I feel really sick.'

Dan came into the kitchen, ready to leave for work. He was on his way to a trade fair that day. He stretched out his arms to Maya and gave her a big hug.

'Good luck! Do call me at the fair as soon as you get your grades. I am sure they will be fine. Remember, we know how hard you have worked. You have done your best. You are our star.'

Maya was near to tears. She loved her parents, despite all their bickering.

****

Amy and Maya were very soon on the familiar road to Milchester. The journey took longer than normal because of traffic congestion. Maya was getting anxious, fingering her hair and constantly looking at her watch. Amy tried to cheer her up as they drove at a snail's pace through the suburbs.

'Just think, Maya, you will soon be starting a new life at uni... new friends and a new chapter in London. You can't do much better than that.'

'Hmmm,' replied Maya, grumpily, 'that's only if I get the right grades.'

There followed a long silence as they drove their way through the slow-moving traffic.

'Can't we get a move on?' urged Maya. 'We are going to be late, and I have arranged to meet Laura so we can pick up the results together.'

Amy was getting exasperated. 'I am doing my very best, Maya. I can't go any faster in this traffic. I'm sure Laura will wait for you to open her envelope.'

Eventually, they reached the college, which was bursting with students and parents. Maya phoned Laura.

'I am just about to go into the hall now,' Laura said, on the other end of the phone. 'I am by the doors. Oh my God, I am shaking.'

'Yes, I think I can see you,' replied Maya. 'Yes I can now.'

And so the two girls moved towards each other and joined the crowded crush of students heading into the main hall to collect results envelopes. There was an air of nervous excitement punctuated by cries and occasional screams of delight as students received their results. They decided that Laura would be the first of the two of them to open her envelope.

'Oh no. Here we go,' she groaned, and her fingers trembled as she opened it. 'Yes, but… oh no… hang on. Oh yes!' Laura screamed with excitement as she scanned the results. 'Yes, yes, yes! I have got all the grades I need.'

Laura had got the grades for her place at the Olivier Drama College in Leeds. The two girls hugged. Now it was Maya's turn to open her envelope. She slowly opened it, read it, mumbling and shaking her head. Laura feared the worst. Surely Maya hadn't failed? She was such a clever girl.

'Come on, Maya, tell me what you've got,' exclaimed Laura.

'Hang on, give me a chance,' Maya exclaimed and then, after a dramatic pause, 'Yes! I'm through. I've got the grades I need. London here I come. I am so very, very happy.'

Both girls were squealing with excitement and hugging each other. They moved back through the crowded hall, sharing their good news with friends as they did so.

'I must tell Mum,' said Maya, who in all the excitement had forgotten that her mother was just outside the hall, together with Laura's mother, Fiona. The girls soon found them.

'We are both through,' said Laura excitedly.

'We have got our grades,' confirmed Maya, still in a state of shock.

After congratulations and hugs had been exchanged, Amy texted Dan with the good news.

'Why don't we all go out for a celebration drink and a bite to eat? How about a pizza at La Toscana?' she then suggested.

'Sounds good to me,' agreed Fiona.

Ten minutes later, they arrived at the restaurant. Other students and their parents were already sitting at other tables, laughing, drinking and loudly celebrating their success. The waiter approached their table and took an order for pizzas all round.

'How about some bubbles for you students?' he asked, smiling at the two girls. 'You have both passed your exams, I guess?'

'Yes, yes. Thank you,' they nodded their heads and smiled at him.

'Congratulations!' he replied. 'I will bring you all a glass of our celebration prosecco – it's on the house.'

The wine and pizzas soon arrived. They were all in good spirits and time flew past. But eventually and reluctantly the two mothers decided that they should set off for home to spread the good news to more friends and family.

Amy and Maya got into the car. Maya then started texting her other mates as Amy rapidly drove off. Maya was wondering if her mother was within the legal alcohol limit. Of course she was, she told herself. She must be. It was results day.

When Maya had got home she disappeared upstairs into her bedroom and, after texting and chatting to friends for a while, fell into a deep sleep.

****

Dan eventually arrived later that evening with a bag that clinked as he put it down on the kitchen table.

'You are our big star,' he exclaimed as he gave a hug to Maya who had now come downstairs after her sleep. 'We are so proud of you.' Dan gingerly took a bottle of prosecco out of his bag, exclaiming, 'Surprise! Surprise!'

He looked at Amy and Maya, and saw that they were exchanging glances.

'Don't tell me,' he exclaimed. 'You have already been out to celebrate.'

'Sorry, Dan,' replied Amy. 'We did put our nose into La Toscana for a pizza and drinks.'

'And I'm heading out tonight with Laura to celebrate,' Maya added.

'No problem,' he replied, laughing. 'We have plenty of time to drink this later.'

Dan then remembered that he had not yet told his father, Ollie, about Maya's success. His father was very fond of his granddaughter and would want to know. Dan decided to phone him early the following day when it would be early evening in Australia.

The plan for that evening had been that Maya and Laura and other friends would meet up in the Pilgrim Club in Milchester to celebrate. The Pilgrim was a popular haunt for students to drink and dance the night away. This time it was Dan's turn to drive Maya to the party.

On arrival Maya soon spotted Laura who was on her own.

'Where's Nick then?' asked Maya.

'Oh, he's working on some gig out of town. It often happens. Worse luck.'

The two of them headed inside and were soon dancing together, but Laura kept looking around the dance floor as if she was searching for someone and it began to irritate Maya.

'What's up with you?' asked Maya. 'What's going on? Who are you looking for?'

'Oh, sorry,' replied Laura. 'I was waiting for someone to join us, but he hasn't turned up.'

'It's a *he*, then?' asked Maya with a big grin on her face. 'Sounds interesting!'

At this point Laura's phone started to vibrate and she left Maya to dance on her own. Maya carried on dancing for a while, carefully watching Laura in deep conversation on her phone by the bar. Maya was wondering what was going on. Who was it that Laura had invited to join them? Maya stopped dancing and walked over to her.

'What's up, Laura?' she asked. 'Any sign of this guy you were talking about?'

'Oh, yes,' replied Laura, trying to hide the big smile on her face. 'He's an old mate of mine who happens to be around today. His parents live in London but he's visiting family here. I have just heard from him. He should be with us very soon.'

'I hope he is a good-looker,' replied Maya, grinning at Laura.

A couple of minutes later Maya spotted a fair-haired young man approaching the bar. She watched him closely. She thought that he was rather good-looking. Then to her surprise Laura waved him over to where they were standing.

'Hi, James, glad to see you made it!' she exclaimed as he joined them at the bar. She then turned to introduce him to Maya. 'This is James, a good friend. He got his results today, too. Tell Maya your good news, James.'

'I am going to study Law at UCL,' he replied in a deep and rather posh voice.

As he spoke he kept eye contact with Maya, who was listening intently.

'And Maya has also got the grades she needs to get into uni in London. She's a clever girl.'

'Hi James,' said Maya, rather overwhelmed by it all. 'It's good to meet you.'

'Errrm. Why don't we all get some drinks here and grab a table?' Laura suggested.

'Good plan, Laura,' replied James.

The threesome then moved to a table away from the bar. Maya was clearly captivated by James and was soon telling him about her university course.

'Yes, yes. I am going to London as well,' said Maya, feeling herself blushing. 'To study English Lit at Maynard College. It's in north London.' She paused as she looked at him straight in the eyes. 'So, what made you choose law, James?'

'Well, I wanted to follow in my father's footsteps. He's a lawyer in the City, you know. Specialises in commercial law.'

And so the conversation continued. Laura watched as Maya and James began to get on really well together. She smiled to herself. All she needed to do now was to leave them on their own for a while. After they had finished their drinks, she explained where she was heading.

'Sorry, guys, I have to go home now. It is a shame but my mother is picking me up very soon. And so…' she paused with a grin spreading over her face, 'that means that you two can dance the night away. So goodbye! Goodnight! And have a great time.'

Maya and James both gave Laura a big hug and she disappeared into the crowd. They then sat down and looked at each other over the table. Maya was the first to speak.

'Perhaps… maybe we could… errrr?'

'Dance?' suggested James, smiling.

They moved over to the dance floor and were soon dancing as if they had known each other for a long time. As the music gradually slowed down, they were moving closer and closer together. Laura's plan had worked.

'Why don't we sit down somewhere again?' asked James when the music stopped.

'Good plan,' replied Maya. 'It's a bit noisy here, don't you think?'

They found another table in a quiet corner and started to compare notes about the schools they had gone to and their plans for university life in London. After a while there was a pause in the conversation as both of them wondered what to say next. Their eyes met over the table. James was the first to speak.

'Maybe we can meet up again?' he asked. Maya melted.

'Yes… that would be good,' she replied.

'It's been a super evening, Maya. Thanks so much. I really do hope I will see you again. And soon. How are you getting home?'

'It has been great for me too,' replied Maya, flashing her dark eyes at him. 'My dad will be here soon to pick me up. Errr, yes… in fact… would you like a lift?'

'Many thanks, Maya, but I am not far from my uncle's place here. Just walking distance in fact. I will definitely make sure you get safely to your dad's car, though.'

Maya looked at him with a winning gleam in her eyes. After Luke's thoughtlessness, James's chivalry was refreshing. 'Maybe we should exchange phone numbers?' she said.

'Great idea,' replied James and they swapped numbers. 'Let's get you to your dad and safely home.'

They both stood up. She moved around the table so that they were standing face to face. Maya took his hands in hers, looked up at him, pulled him towards her and leaned in to kiss him. When he responded, Maya was in seventh heaven.

Outside the club, Maya could see her father's car waiting at the top of the road. She and James walked slowly and reluctantly towards him. She didn't want the evening to end. Dan wound down the window and peered out at his daughter and the young man she was with.

'Dad,' Maya said, shyly, 'this is James. He's a friend of Laura's and we just met tonight.'

'Nice to meet you, James,' Dan said, impressed. 'And thank you for making sure Maya got to the car safely.' He winked at Maya who blushed.

'No problem, Mr Barnes,' James said, squeezing Maya's hand before letting it go. 'Maya, I'll call you.'

Maya slid into the car next to her dad and watched James walk away in the rearview mirror.

'He seems nice,' Dan said, smiling.

'He really is, Dad,' Maya said. Her heart was still fluttering.

Back at the cottage, Amy was still awake and Maya had to tell her mother all about her new catch, James.

'Oh, Mum, I met a lovely guy tonight. He is a bit posh but we get on really well. He's going to call me. And he's going to be studying in London this autumn.'

'That's wonderful,' Amy said. She glanced at Dan who gave a small nod.

'He does indeed seem to be a very nice boy,' Dan said.

'But I really should get to bed soon,' Maya said, yawning.

'No problem,' said Amy. 'But first, how about a hug?'

Maya hugged her mother and bounded upstairs.

In her bedroom, Maya just had to call Laura.

'Laura... I don't know how to thank you for introducing me to James. You are a real treasure. He is really lovely.'

'He seemed to be very keen on you, too' replied Laura. 'And don't you think he is very good-looking? Yes? Really fit don't you think? You have scored there, Maya, my girl. I'm so pleased for you. Anyway, I'll talk to you tomorrow.'

After the conversation Maya snuggled down in her bed, but she really could not sleep. She had only one person in her mind. His name was James. She longed to see him again.

Chapter 11

The start of the university autumn term was getting closer and closer. Maya had been counting down the weeks since her exam results and was both excited and anxious about leaving home. There was a lot to think about. What would Maynard College be like to live in? Would the work be difficult? And last, but not least… when would she be able to meet up with James again?

They had been in almost constant contact since meeting at the club. He had returned to his parents' home in London but it was just a matter of weeks before Maya would also be in the city. In her last phone conversation with him he had told her he was going on a short late holiday with his parents to Sorrento, an Italian seaside resort they regularly visited in late August when the noisy crowds had gone away. Soon after he arrived there, he had sent Maya colourful postcards of the Italian coast, all of them signed off 'Love from James xxxx See you soon, I hope xxxx!' But for the past week she had not received any more phone messages, which was odd and disappointing. Amy kept reassuring her daughter that James seemed keen and that she should be patient and wait for his next call.

Maya getting ready for uni meant that her mother was also very busy. Amy helped with packing up her belongings, included books, laptop computer, smart clothes, casual clothes, gym kit, running shoes, ordinary shoes, posh shoes, a kettle, and of course her teddy bear. The day came for the journey to London and Dan's spacious Land Rover was nearly full. And he was getting cross.

'How the hell am I to get all this in my car? And two passengers as well?'

'Don't be silly, Dan,' said Amy quietly as if she were talking to a five-year-old. 'We'll make it all fit. Amy needs this stuff.'

Dan snorted in exasperation.

Amy shook her head but kept quiet. The two of them both knew that this was the end of an era. Amy was already considering how it would feel for the two of them to return to the house without Maya later that day. Just the two of them…

At long last, everything that needed to go in the car was in the car and Dan was driving them to the city. As the journey progressed, he was getting more and more irritated with Amy tapping away on her phone, and Maya listening to music – earphones firmly lodged in her ears.

After what seemed like an eternity, they reached Maynard College in the Hampstead area of north London. It was buzzing with activity as students and parents converged for a day of family farewells.

Maya had been given a small and cosy upstairs

room in Tennyson Hall, a student hall of residence not far from the main university buildings. While they were moving Maya's seemingly endless stuff up into her room, she met the girl who had been allocated the room next to hers. They had a brief chat together. Her name was Anwen and she was Welsh, with a strong accent and long dark hair. Maya took an immediate liking to her. She reckoned that she was going to enjoy being at Maynard College.

Before long, the time arrived for Dan and Amy to say their goodbyes. Maya accompanied them back to the car and they both gave her a big farewell hug, Amy and Maya were both in tears and Dan was also feeling choked up about leaving his precious girl in a big city.

After Dan and Amy had driven off, waving goodbye to their daughter, they knew that a family milestone had been passed. They were now on their own. Just the two of them with daggers drawn. Dan wondered seriously about their future as they set out on the long journey back home. Neither of them spoke to the other, except when Amy helpfully told Dan that eighty miles an hour was exceeding the speed limit on the motorway.

Meanwhile at Maynard College, Maya made her way back to her new room and started to unpack her books and clothes, but soon got tired of it all. She was still upset about saying goodbye to her parents. And she was worried about what would become of their relationship now she was away from home. She could hear Anwen's voice in the corridor, followed by her door shutting and the sound of her moving around in the room next door. Impulsively, Maya grabbed a jar of coffee and walked out into the passage and knocked on her neighbour's door, which slowly opened revealing Anwen's face.

'Fancy a coffee?' asked Maya attempting to put on a cheery voice and a happy face. She held up the jar.

'Well yes, goodness me, sure do,' replied Anwen, her whole face lighting up.

'Well, why don't you come and check out my room?' asked Maya.

And so it was that the two girls soon got to know each other. They exchanged notes on what they were going to study, where they had grown up, their parents, and their boyfriends. Anwen was at uni to study psychology. She had recently split with her boyfriend and was looking forward to meeting other boys in London.

Maya told Anwen about herself, but didn't mention her recent split from Luke. He was very much off the radar. But she did mention that she had met a boy called James who was starting a law degree at University College, London.

'Sounds promising!' exclaimed Anwen. 'Have you known him for long? Is he really fit? Are things serious between you?'

'No, not yet,' replied Maya. 'I have only met him once and I don't really know him properly – although we did kiss. But you never know what might happen now we are both in London. He is rather lovely.'

And so the two girls chatted away, finding that they had a lot in common.

****

After supper in the refectory Maya and Anwen visited the Students' Union bar. They were gasping for a drink, and needed to relax after the emotional turmoil of the day. Anwen also wanted to suss out the new male students.

Anwen soon had her sights set on a certain boy at the bar who seemed to be on his own. She left Maya and sidled up near to him, glancing at him and trying to catch his eye. Another girl suddenly appeared at his other side. She put her hand on his shoulder and they started chatting as they drank. And so Anwen gave up and returned to a bored looking Maya who had become weary of Anwen's boy chasing.

'Why don't we call it a night, Anwen?' she suggested. 'I really do need to get some beauty sleep.'

But Anwen did not give up so easily and so they agreed that she should carry on with her manhunt. Maya was more than happy to go back to her new room in Tennyson Hall. She badly wanted to talk to her parents. She got through to them straightaway on her return.

'Hi, it's me!' she said. 'Can you put this on speakerphone? I am in my uni room on my own.'

'Yes, sure, will do! Is everything OK?' asked Amy anxiously.

'Yeah. You bet. All going good here. My room is a bit cramped with all the stuff I brought, but it's cosy.'

'So, what have you been up to today?' asked Amy.

'Well, I have unpacked, or tried to, and we've been to the bar tonight.'

'With Anwen?' asked Amy.

'Yeah, I'm getting on pretty well with Anwen. She is really lovely.' Maya paused. 'You know, I think she is going to be a really good friend.'

'That's great,' remarked Dan.

'Of course. We had a drink or two. But…' Maya paused.

'But what?' asked Dan. It was his turn to sound concerned.

'Anwen is very keen on chatting up the boys. A bit too keen, I think. She's still down there at the bar. I came back to my room and am now in bed. I'm so tired.' She paused and yawned loudly. 'Sorry! I really think I need some sleep. I just wanted to say goodnight and that I love you both. And I am missing you already. You are both such a help and support for me.' Maya was becoming tearful.

'Love you too, Maya,' replied Dan. 'I think you are going to have a great time at uni.'

'Missing you lots already, too,' said Amy, who was also welling up. 'Do keep us posted.'

'OK, Mum. I will. I promise.'

Maya turned off her phone and looked around her room. She had found herself in a completely different world. It all felt very strange.

****

The following morning, Maya decided to head down to the refectory for breakfast. She was about to see whether Anwen wanted to join her when she remembered that her Welsh friend may have had a late night visitor – if she had snared one. And so Maya carried on down to the refectory alone.

After breakfast she returned to her room to make a coffee and finish sorting out her books and other belongings before she headed in for her first lecture. There was a knock on her door. She opened it gingerly. Anwen stood there, looking washed out.

'Can I come in for a minute?' she asked.

'Yeah, sure. I didn't see you at breakfast. Everything OK?'

'Yeah, just knackered,' replied Anwen. She yawned.

'Cup of coffee? I've made some,' said Maya.

'That would be great,' replied Anwen.

'Anyway,' asked Maya, as she poured the coffee, 'how did you get on last night?'

'There was a boy I really fancied, but he seemed to be a bit on the kinky side. So I left him alone and chatted to some others.'

'Anwen,' said Maya, 'do you ever stop chatting up these boys?'

Anwen did not answer immediately but grinned at Maya. 'I am Welsh, you know,' she eventually said. 'We have hot blood in our veins.'

Maya shook her head, and then burst into laughter. Anwen was definitely going to be a good friend.

****

A few days later, after lectures and seminars had started, Maya was in her room anxiously checking her phone for a message from James. She hadn't heard from him since she received his postcards from Italy. She decided to take the plunge, picked up her phone and started to write a message:

'I hope you had a great holiday in Italy. I am now settled down at Maynard College. Fancy a drink somewhere when you are settled in UCL? Hope to hear from you and see you very soon. xxxx.'

She pressed send and wondered when she would hear from him. It was late in the evening so maybe tomorrow. Maya decided to get started to settle down to get some sleep. But she couldn't help thinking about the first meeting with James – his face, his voice, and the brief kiss they had shared at the pub. She desperately wanted to see him again.

Half an hour later a sleepy Maya was roused by a noise from her phone. It was a reply from James. Suddenly, Maya was now fully awake and her hands shook as she read his message. She could remember hearing his smooth velvety voice.

'Thanks so much for your message. I'm so glad you got in touch. I was going to message you from Italy, but my phone broke. I had it mended but I lost all my numbers. I was so gutted because I thought I had lost your number. I was about to ask Laura for your number again so I was so pleased to see your message. It really would be great to meet up sometime soon. Maybe this Friday? There is a bar called Aphrodite in Russell Square which would be good. Just let me know. xxxx'

Maya looked at the time on her phone. It was nearing midnight. She couldn't help but be pleased that he had replied so quickly. Her brain was now in a rapid spin as she responded to the message. She was aching for him.

****

That Friday evening, Maya met up with James at the Aphrodite bar. She soon spotted him after entering the bar, because he stood up and waved her to his table. She sat down and they ordered some drinks and food. Maya studied him closely as they started to chat. It seemed such a long time since she had last seen him but she still felt the same excitement at seeing him – his stubbly beard, blue eyes and Italian sun tan – and, of course, hearing his smooth velvety voice.

'Well, Maya, it is lovely to see you again. How have you settled in at Maynard?'

'Fine, thank you! I have made some good friends, including a guy-crazy Welsh girl in the room next to mine.'

'Gosh… that must be annoying.'

'No, she's OK really,' replied Maya. 'Except that she can be noisy when she has a visitor in her room late at night.' She grinned at him knowingly. James returned the smile and changed the subject.

'So, how are you enjoying your studies at uni? It's English you are studying? Am I right?'

'Yes, that's right. English Literature,' replied Maya, staring at his handsome face. 'And your law classes have started?'

'Oh yes,' James said. 'Our schedule is really busy but I am enjoying the lectures and I have a great tutor.'

'And you must be specialising in commercial law if that's the area you want to work in.'

'Yes. We have a family legacy of legal eagles so that's the field I intend to work in.'

As the meal progressed they both exchanged more

stories about themselves including about their time at school and their families. James had enjoyed school. He was an only child. His father was a director at the commercial law firm he worked at. His mother didn't work as she was often unwell – she suffered from Multiple Sclerosis – and so family life was sometimes rather difficult. His mother would go through good and bad times with her condition and whilst the family could afford carers for her when she was very poorly, Maya got the impression that James was under a lot of pressure to help at home. James didn't mention any girlfriends and Maya began to wonder if he had ever had the opportunity for a serious relationship with a girl. Maybe she could help him in that department.

'I broke up with my boyfriend over the summer,' Maya confessed. 'He was a big mistake. It took me a while to realise he was bad for me. What about you? Any serious girlfriends?'

'Errr, there was this girl that I really liked from another school. But my parents weren't keen on her. They were keen to get me to start up a relationship with a girl who looked like a horse. It was an absolute nightmare. So, no. No serious relationships really.'

They had finished eating and James suddenly seemed pre-occupied with his phone. This puzzled Maya.

'I am so very sorry,' James said, noting her expression, 'I've just had a message from my mother. Unfortunately Dad has had to fly off to the firm's Paris office and our carer is off sick so my mother needs help at home. I'll have to head back home tonight and get back to campus early tomorrow for my lectures.'

Maya shook her head sadly, caught hold of his hands over the table and looked at him straight in the eyes:

'It's OK, James. I do understand. You need to be there for your mother. That's how things are. It's bound to be difficult for you.'

'I'm really sorry we have to cut the night short.'

'At least let me come with you to the Tube station?' pleaded Maya.

'Yes, of course,' replied James.

James insisting on paying for the meal and they left the bar together. They were soon walking, hand in hand, down a street past a public square full of trees. It was getting dark. And Maya could wait no longer. She tugged at his arm and they passed through the gates and in among the trees. They came to a stop and she put her arms around him, pulling him closer and closer. Feeling him against her, she kissed him – deep and sweet. James responded, losing his inhibitions. Nothing was said. Nothing needed to be said.

Eventually, James gently pulled himself away from Maya's arms and again looked at his watch.

'Sorry, Maya, I really must go now.'

'But I will see you soon,' she said encouragingly. 'We must meet again. Promise?'

'I promise,' was the reply.

James gave Maya a final kiss and rushed off to the Tube station. She watched her handsome boy as he looked back at her and blew her a kiss.

Just like in the movies, Maya thought.

Chapter 12

Maya had no problems in settling down in London. She was making new friends and enjoying a blossoming relationship with James. Dan and Amy, on the other hand, had less rosy perspectives on their future. They both understood that their one and only child had left the nest. Now it was just the two of them alone in their cottage.

The day after they had returned to Birch Cottage, Dan set off on a woodland walk to help clear his mind before the light died away. There was a hint of autumn in the evening air. 'What's next for us?' was the thought that dominated his mind. Would he and Amy be able to work out their differences? Or would there be domestic disintegration? Was she seeing someone else – as he suspected? Would she leave him?

While Dan was out walking and thinking, Amy was clearing up Maya's bedroom. It was in a total mess. Amy felt upset, tired and lonely. Something needed to change in her world. She couldn't keep living like this. Knowing that Dan would not come back for a while, she decided to take a break from the tidying to call Adam. She left Maya's chaos for the comfort of her own bedroom where she lay on the bed clutching her phone. She loved the privacy and the intimacy of her own space.

Adam picked up her call. 'Amy, I'm really glad you called but I am still at work and have a client who is about to arrive in five minutes. Can we be quick?'

Amy got straight to the point.

'I just wanted to let you know that we took Maya to London yesterday. The journey back was total hell – just Dan and I coming back together. He's gone out for a walk. And here I am home alone. And all I wanted was to hear your voice. Can we meet to talk soon? I can't go on like this.'

'I'm glad to hear your voice too. And yes, I want to talk about us and our future together,' he said, but then he broke off the conversation and the line became muffled. She could hear someone talking to him – perhaps they had just come into his office. Then he came back on the line. 'Sorry about that, Amy,' he said. 'But I'll see you in a while at the drinks for the cast, right?' Adam terminated the call.

Adam was a lawyer and Amy could picture him in his smart suit standing up to greet his client with a firm handshake, professional smile and his well-brushed, slightly greying hair. He really was a catch.

Amy thought about the night when she and Adam had gone beyond playful flirting. It was months ago but it was still so memorable. They both had roles in the Milchester Players' production of *As You Like It*. She had been given the role of Rosalind and she certainly did 'like it' as Adam was her male lead. He had made an imposing Orlando, handsome in a mature way with a dramatic voice which made her hair stand on end.

During rehearsals, the two of them had become more and more friendly, and they soon realised that they were on the same wavelength and very much attracted to each other. Late one evening, after a particularly long and tiring rehearsal, the cast was in desperate need of a drink and decided to head to the nearby King Charles pub. Adam quietly suggested that the two of them head to another pub he knew where they could be alone. She readily agreed and they walked to the nearby Talbot pub.

They had chatted over drinks, and Amy mentioned to him that Dan was away on business in Frankfurt and Maya was away from home, staying with friends after a party. By the time last orders were called they had downed their gin and tonics. Time had flown by.

Outside the pub Adam put his arm around Amy's shoulders and asked her back to his apartment on the top floor of an up-market block. Amy hadn't hesitated in her answer. She could remember it all so clearly. He had a balcony overlooking the River Avon. More drinks were poured and predictably she had found herself in his bed, stroking his hair and feeling his smooth soft hands all over her.

A night to remember.

But Amy's thoughts of the past were suddenly interrupted by the sound of their front door opening and then shouting. Dan had returned home from his walk.

'Amy, I need to talk to you,' he shouted, assuming that Amy was on her phone upstairs as usual. Amy stood up, looked in the mirror and composed herself before heading downstairs where she picked up her car keys. It was a little too early to leave for the drinks but she really didn't want to talk to Dan.

'Not now. I just need to pop into Milchester for the monthly social meeting of the players. I'll be back soon.'

Dan seemed annoyed.

'Why didn't you tell me that Matt called us yesterday from Sydney?' he asked. 'He has just messaged me. He said he really wants to talk. He said you picked up yesterday on the house phone and he left a message.'

Amy gasped. She had forgotten to pass on the message.

'Oh my God! I forgot to tell you. He couldn't get through to you on your mobile for some reason or other. Look, I'm sorry, Dan. I guess I was distracted with worrying about Maya settling in. I don't think it's urgent. He said your dad was fine but he just wanted to speak to you about something.'

Dan looked at Amy, his face as black as thunder. He hadn't spoken to his brother since Sophie's death. He'd left so many messages and written letters and they had all gone unanswered. In his heart he knew that his brother blamed him for the death of Sophie. And he also blamed himself. The nightmares had not stopped. He could still see Sophie floating in that dark water in his dreams.

'Well, it rather looks like I'm stuffed. It's now the middle of the night in Sydney,' he said wearily. 'Oh shit. I will have to wait and call him tomorrow morning.'

Dan went into the living room on his own and put the TV on to calm the storm. Amy left in her car.

****

When Amy returned late that evening she found Dan in the living room. He had already knocked back several glasses of wine.

'Look. I'm sorry about forgetting to tell you Matt had called,' she said. 'I was so preoccupied with making sure Maya was settled. I'm sure your dad is fine. Matt would have said if it was something urgent.'

'My brother hasn't returned my messages for months,' Dan said angrily, still watching the TV screen. 'Amy, if you cared even a little bit, you would have passed that message on right away.'

'I've said I'm sorry,' she said before turning and heading upstairs to the bathroom. As she washed her face, she thought about how long it had been since the two of them had got close and personal with each other or even slept in the same bed. She remembered her early years with him, raunchy weekends in Woodham B&Bs and red hot sessions in the cottage when Maya was little. When she returned to check on him, she found him quietly snoring and passed out. She removed the half-empty glass of wine from his grasp, carefully propped him up with cushions and covered him with a blanket to keep him warm. After a minute more of remembering the past, Amy quietly left, closed the sitting room door and slowly headed upstairs alone to her bed and its cold sheets. Something had to change.

****

The following morning, Dan woke on the sofa. He felt groggy from last night's wine and vaguely remembered the harsh words with Amy. But he was anxious to make the phone call to Matt in Australia. His phone was on the coffee table in front of him. He dialled the number.

'Hi, Dan. Thanks for calling me back.' Matt sounded distant and detached.

'Matt, I was so pleased to hear you called,' Dan said. 'What's happening?'

Matt cleared his throat and continued, 'Lisa and I are here in Sydney, visiting Dad.'

'Is he OK?' asked Dan.

'He is in good spirits but recently his health has not been what it was. We organised for him to see his doctor who referred him to a specialist. We saw the specialist two days ago and we have a diagnosis.'

'What is it?' asked Dan.

'It's Parkinson's Disease,' replied Matt. 'Not good news. It explains why he's had issues with shaky hands and slow movements. The specialist also said it can cause depression and other issues. He's going to need special care going forward.'

There was then a long pause as both Dan and Matt both wondered what to say next. Sophie's drowning was the tragedy that hung, unspoken, between them. Neither of them wanted to talk about it.

'Understood,' Dan said to break the silence. 'We'll

do whatever he needs. Thanks for letting me know. And Matt, it's good to hear from you. How have you been? I—'

Then the line went completely dead and there was just silence. Dan felt broken. He knew that the searing pain of Sophie's death remained with his brother and with Lisa. And there was nothing he could say or do to change it.

Chapter 13

It was an autumnal Saturday, and the evening was closing in around Birch Cottage. The sun was sinking low in the sky making a golden display of the autumn trees before fading into dark shadows. Dan was at home, sprawled out on the sofa in the living room with a bottle of wine. He was deep in thought.

It had been more than a month since Maya had left home for a new life at uni. Now that she had gone, Dan and Amy's fragile relationship had really started to fall apart. Dan felt trapped in the cottage. He was often annoyed by Amy's critical remarks and her irritating chatter on the phone to her friends. And he was more convinced than ever that she was having an affair.

His brother hadn't called again since he had delivered the news about their father's diagnosis. Dan had spoken to his father a few times but he really missed his brother. He knew that his twinwas holding him responsible for the death of his niece and Dan didn't know how on earth they would ever reconcile.

And yet, the most significant loss for Dan was Maya. He missed her. He missed their chats about school and helping with her homework – especially maths. Now it seemed to him that it was mainly Amy who provided advice and guidance to their daughter in London. Maya was brief and bubbly with him on the phone but it seemed to be her mother that she confided in.

He knew that he and Amy were heading for disaster. Something was bound to happen to end their relationship. And soon. But how would Maya react if he and Amy split up? No doubt Amy would convince Maya that it was all his fault. He wouldn't be able to win.

He took a slurp of wine and got up from the sofa. Time was ticking on and he could hear Amy upstairs in her room buzzing about like a manic wasp, getting ready for her regular Friday evening rehearsal with the Milchester Players. The latest production was another Shakespeare play – *Romeo and Juliet*. Amy was playing the role of Juliet and Dan knew that a guy called Adam had been cast as Romeo. Dan chuckled to himself. Amy was closing in on her forties and he was certain that this guy, Adam, couldn't be much younger. They were both old enough in real life to be the lovers' parents. It was just crazy casting. Dan poured another glass of wine.

Amy eventually came rushing downstairs and popped her head around the living room door.

'I'll be back late.'

'OK, Amy,' replied Dan sarcastically. 'Have a lovely time. Give my regards to Romeo. See you later… or not, as may be.'

'What the fuck is that supposed to mean?' she asked angrily.

'You bloody well know what I mean. I know you've been flirting with guys at that drama group.' Amy gave him an angry glare but he was more angry. 'And anyway, who's ever heard of Juliet being played by a middle-aged woman? Are you really up to the role?'

Amy shook her head, muttering something, probably unrepeatable, under her breath. She made her way through the front door, slamming it behind her.

After settling back on the sofa Dan looked to see what was on the TV – anything to take his mind off the current situation. He chose a programme about sheepdogs. He thought it was good to see animals that did what they were told to do, with unconditional loyalty to their owner. The dogs shared a mutual affection with their owners – something that was badly missing in his own life.

Ten minutes later and after another glass of wine, he was fast asleep.

****

The following morning Dan woke on the sofa again. He threw together a plateful of scrambled eggs and bacon. There was no sign of Amy. He hadn't even heard her come home. Had she gone out again before he woke up? Perhaps she had stayed out all night. Strangely, Dan began to feel relaxed that he was alone. The Sunday paper arrived, pushed through the letterbox where it landed with a great thump on the mat. Dan picked it up and gave it a cursory glance as he sat down at the kitchen table. The 'What's on' section in the paper was promoting a new series starting on the BBC covering the anguish of separation and divorce and the effect on families with children. Dan pushed the paper to one side. That was all too close to home.

Dan looked out through the cottage window and saw that it was an ideal day for a walk. On passing through the front gate he noticed that Amy's car was not on the drive. If she had come home last night, she had left again. Good riddance, he thought. He was soon on his way and after an hour of striding through the woods he reached the river and followed the path next to it, the recent rains dangerously swirling below him in a treacherous muddy torrent. He couldn't help but think of that dreadful day at the top of the hill and, feeling rather sick, he turned back and made his way home.

On his way back to the cottage, he passed through a glade of beech trees, the leaves of which had turned from green to glorious tones of russet and gold and were now starting to fall. The afternoon then passed by pleasantly and uneventfully.

At 8 o'clock in the evening, Amy had still not returned. Dan needed to let her know that the following day he was going to a kitchen exhibition in Oxford where he would be on the Leichmatic stall. He called her mobile and she picked up straightaway but it was noisy where she was and he found it difficult to hear what she was saying. It sounded like she was at a very lively gathering.

'Amy. Where are you?'

'I'm in Milchester again,' Amy's speech was a little

slurred. 'A bunch of us from the players were invited to a party at one of Adam's colleagues.'

'Did you even come home last night?' Dan asked.

'I did but it was late and you were asleep snoring on the sofa. You were still there when I left this morning. I thought about leaving you a note but I forgot.'

'So when will you be back?' asked Dan casually.

'Not sure about that.' There was a pause. Amy seemed to be speaking to someone else at the same time.

'Hello? Amy? Are you there?' Dan was getting very irritated.

'Yes, I'm still here,' replied Amy. 'Don't know about when I'll be back. Looks like this party may go on late and so I may need to stay over.'

'Fine. I'm going to Oxford tomorrow for work. And I'm staying overnight so I won't be home until the following day. I guess I'll see you when I see you.' Dan hung up. He knew that there was absolutely nothing that he could do. He turned off his phone, and settled down in front of the TV. He was soon taken into another world as he watched an old black and white wartime film.

He decided to have an early night. He had woken up on the sofa a few too many times lately. Sitting up in bed checking through his work diary, he noted that the kitchen show started at ten o'clock and so he would need to be there by 9.30 to ensure everything was set up. He had arranged to stay overnight after the show with a school friend, Alex, who lived in a nearby village and who rather enjoyed his beer. He was looking forward to a night away from the cottage and hopefully a good chat with old friend.

After a relatively good night's sleep, he woke to find that Amy hadn't come home, as expected. He made an early start and was soon driving through the familiar Cotswold countryside. It was raining hard and Dan was listening to music which he was struggling to hear over the loud swish-clunk of his windscreen wipers. But he felt relatively relaxed as he entered the Oxford suburbs and arrived at the conference centre. By now, he almost did not care what Amy was up to.

Dan loved conference days. They provided a chance to catch up with Leichmatic colleagues and enjoy lunchtime beer and sandwiches.

This year the main gossip over lunch was about the UK sales figures. His earlier conversation with Schneider in Frankfurt was now common knowledge. Everybody knew that the UK was underperforming and there was a real fear about whether there would be redundancies. Nobody seemed to know about the possibility of the merger though. Dan kept quiet about what he knew and put it to the back of his mind. He had a daughter at university and his relationship was disintegrating, he could not afford to be made redundant.

The conference wound up in the late afternoon and as he headed to his car, Dan received a call on his phone. It was Alex.

'Dan, hi. Listen, mate, sorry but I've come down with something. I am not at all well and feel absolutely rubbish. I think it may have been a dodgy curry I had last night but it could also be a virus and so will be catching.'

'Oh no,' replied Dan, inwardly cursing. 'I am so sorry to hear that.'

'Can you find somewhere else to stay tonight? If I were you I wouldn't come anywhere near me at the moment.'

'I think I'll probably just drive home,' replied Dan. He had only drunk one beer at lunch so he was fine to drive back. 'Sounds awful. I hope you get over it soon. Message me when you are better and we will see if we can fix up another date? Sorry again... it sounds a real bugger.'

Dan wondered about texting Amy to tell her he would be home early but he decided not to. She hadn't seen the need to tell him where she was the last couple of nights so why should he bother? Dan arrived back at Birch Cottage in the late evening. He had been wondering what sort of reception he would get from Amy or if she would even be at home. He got a shock as he pulled into the driveway. There was a gleaming silver Jaguar sports car parked next to Amy's little blue runabout. Dan immediately thought of the rich lawyer, Adam, who would be the only person Amy knew with pots of money to spend on a car like that.

Dan parked his car next to the other two and approached the cottage. He was already steaming with anger and only just resisted the temptation to run his keys over the Jaguar's paintwork. He opened the front door. All was quiet in the cottage. What was going on? He quietly entered the kitchen. There was evidence on the table of a hasty meal of cheese and ham rolls, together with an empty bottle of one of his special and rather expensive vintage red wines.

But then something else caught his eye. A large white envelope, propped up against the vase of flowers on the kitchen table. His name was written on it in bold, large handwriting so that he wouldn't miss it. He snatched the envelope and extracted a letter, his fingers trembling. He started to read:

'Dan,

I don't think this will come as a shock. We have both known for a long while that things aren't good between us. I believe the time has come when we can no longer go on together as we are. We need time and space on our own. I will be staying with a friend in Milchester for a while to get my head straight. And so by the time you return and get this letter I will have left. I will call and we can talk about next steps but for now, I need to be by myself.

But please, please, do not mention anything to Maya about all this. She is still finding her feet after leaving home. I don't want to destabilise her right now. We can tell her together when the time is right.

I am so sorry – but we really can't go on like this.

Amy.'

Dan had to sit down and then read the letter again. He was shocked but as Amy had expected, he had to admit that he had seen this coming. And, he realised, she had clearly expected him to find this letter tomorrow after she had left. But she was clearly still here as her car was here. And she probably wasn't alone. Everything suddenly felt strangely hostile in his own cottage. There was no sound to be heard apart from crows cawing hideously in the trees outside. Then Dan could hear movement upstairs.

Seething with anger, he crept silently up the stairs to the landing.

As he reached the top of the stairs, the door to Amy's room suddenly swung open. A silver-haired man wearing one of Amy's dressing gowns appeared. He locked eyes with Dan. Dan froze. Neither of them spoke. Then Amy's voice came from inside the bedroom:

'Come on, Adam. Get a move on and get back in here. For God's sake, shift yourself— What? What is it?'

Amy bustled her way out behind the man. She stopped, looking aghast at Dan as if she had seen a ghost.

'Dan. What are you doing here?'

'I believe I live here, actually,' was Dan's sarcastic reply. All three of them stood, not really knowing what to say. Dan composed himself, then looked at Adam Ashworth. 'Perhaps I should be asking what *you* are doing here. I presume you are the '*friend*' Amy is leaving to stay with.'

'Yes, Dan. I am. I am here to help Amy move out.' Dan gave an angry snort. Adam continued, in a calm voice, as if he was talking to an idiot, 'Look. She didn't want it to happen like this. Just give us half an hour at the most. We have already packed the car with most of her belongings. We'll leave right away.'

At this point Dan lost control.

'How dare you, you smarmy bastard?' He paused, breathing heavily, barely containing his anger. 'I can't believe this... you're fucking Amy in my own home?'

Dan raised his fists and Adam responded in kind. Amy, now in tears, pulled him away from Dan.

'Just leave it, Adam,' she begged. 'We need to get out of here and away from this lunatic. And soon. Please. Dan, I'm leaving. You can't stop me. Don't make this harder than it is.'

Amy pulled Adam into her bedroom, shutting the door firmly. Dan was left alone on the stairway, steaming with anger but realising that she was right – he couldn't stop her. He decided to get out of the way before he did something he might regret. He headed outside and away from the cottage to breathe in some fresh night air. As he passed it, he was again tempted by the idea of scraping his keys down the side of Adam's gleaming Jaguar. He reached into his anorak pocket but then changed his mind. Maybe not such a good idea. He was beginning to cool down as he strode down the path to the woods.

An hour later Dan returned to an empty and quiet cottage. Amy had cleared her clothes from her bedroom and taken other belongings, leaving the cottage in a big mess. She had been in a hurry to get away with her new man. And now Dan was alone.

****

Adam and Amy had left the cottage in a hurry. Adam was glad to get away and Amy was dazed by all that had happened and was wondering if Dan would respect her wishes for them to tell Maya together. He must have known that this day was coming but he had still been so angry. She reassured herself in the knowledge that he had definitely been with someone else in Frankfurt. If anything, he had made the move before she did. Their relationship was over.

They soon arrived at Adam's smart Milchester apartment where Amy unpacked some belongings. They were soon settling down for a rest on his smooth leather sofa, each with a gin and tonic in hand. Amy was weary and confused.

'What is it with Dan, Amy?' asked Adam who was fuming with anger. 'He must have seen this coming? Is he blind? Is he stupid? Is he both? Surely he knew that something had to be going on between you and me.'

Amy spoke quietly and purposefully, 'Well, I always thought he'd guessed. And I'm pretty sure he hasn't been faithful. There was a night he spent in Frankfurt that we never really talked about afterwards. I called his mobile and a woman picked up. But today he was so angry. Between his temper and the drinking, it really is the last straw. I am so sorry you had to go through that.' Amy pulled Adam closer to her on the sofa as she spoke. 'I know we can put it behind us now. Of course we can. After all, we have each other. It's a new beginning for us.'

'Yes, absolutely.'

'But,' she paused, 'I'll have to call him tomorrow. There's still something I need to make sure we've sorted out.'

Adam looked at Amy quizzically. 'And what's that?' he asked. 'You mean *who* is that? I'm thinking about Maya and how we tell her what's happened. I don't want her to hear it from Dan – especially as he's so angry right now. Maybe I should tell her what has happened today.'

'Sounds a no-brainer to me,' replied Adam. 'Maybe you should call her now?'

'Yes, maybe,' said Amy, 'but I really don't really like the idea of that. I think it is important to talk to her face-to-face about this. If I just tell her over the phone she will get very upset.'

'OK then,' replied Adam. 'Fair comment... you have got a good point there. Why don't you call her and organise to meet her in London? And hopefully get ahead of Dan.'

Amy nodded, gave Adam a big kiss and headed into the bedroom to fetch her phone. She messaged Maya and told her she would be coming to London the next day and that she would love to see her. Maya responded almost immediately, excited about the idea of seeing her mother. It didn't appear that she knew about anything that had happened earlier that day. Dan must have refrained from calling her. Amy knew that she had to tell her, though. Face-to-face, she would break the news about her and her father.

'OK then. Give me the verdict!' said Adam, teasing her as she returned to the lounge.

'I've organised to see her tomorrow,' replied Amy, 'but I could do with another drink now.' She flopped back onto the sofa.

'You told her that you had news for her?' asked Adam, pouring her another gin and returning to the sofa.

'No, I just said I would come down to London to see her tomorrow so that we can catch up. I have not told her anything at all about me and Dan and you and me. No way! I must wait until I go and see her and break the news then.'

'That's just what I would do, Amy,' said Adam.

'How about – after these drinks – we grab a pizza from the freezer and demolish a bottle of red wine? And then…' Adam suggested. Amy grinned at her man, and pulled him closer.

'And then an early night for us both, don't you think?' she said.

Adam looked at her and gave her a knowing smile. 'So, why don't we have the pizza afterwards?' he asked.

'Why not indeed?' replied Amy getting to her feet. No more words were necessary. They moved into the bedroom, rapidly tearing off their clothes – hungry for each other.

Chapter 14

Amy slept well that night. Now that she had abandoned her old home for Adam's cosy luxury bedroom overlooking the river in Milchester, she felt totally liberated. It was a new life.

The next morning, she and Adam were fast asleep together in bed. Suddenly, her phone on the bedside table started pinging loudly. Adam woke up and was muttering in annoyance as he looked at his watch.

'For God's sake, Amy, it's only just six o'clock.' he exclaimed. 'Who is calling you?'

'I am so sorry,' said Amy as she grabbed the phone and disappeared into the bathroom to let him get back to sleep. She sat uncomfortably on the edge of the bath and read the message. It was from Maya.

> 'Mum. Where are you? I tried calling home after we messaged yesterday and there was no answer. Is everything OK? So please, please, please can you call me? Love you.'

Amy phoned her back straightaway, silently thanking the powers that be that Dan had not answered the phone at the cottage. He'd probably passed out on the sofa after an inevitable bottle or two of wine.

'Maya, it's me. Everything is fine at home. I wasn't there last night. I'll explain everything today—'

'Mum,' replied Maya. 'Where were you last night? And where was Dad? I seem to be going crazy here. I have been awake for hours and hours with my brain spinning round and round, wondering if everything is OK with you both. I have been so very worried. Things seemed very much on the brink when I left for uni—'

'OK, Maya,' Amy interrupted. 'Listen to me. I really do think it's best to talk this over later today. I'm getting a train into London. Let's meet later and we can talk. OK?'

'OK. Thanks Mum,' replied Maya. 'That would be great. Just hearing your voice makes me feel better already. Love you. See you in a few hours.'

The phone call finished and Amy returned to the bedroom to find Adam wide awake, sitting up in bed. 'What's going on, Amy?'

'Nothing,' she assured him. 'Just Maya getting worried because she called the cottage last night. Thankfully Dan didn't answer. I want to tell her about this myself. It'll be better when I've seen her today and had a chance to tell her what's happened.'

Amy climbed slowly back into bed with him, reached over to his side and negotiated a kiss and cuddle. All was forgiven. Adam loved her wandering fingers.

****

Hours later, Amy set off on her way to London. On the way she rehearsed everything she was going to say to her daughter about her split with Maya's father. There was no doubt in her mind that the split had to happen. It had been inevitable. But how to break the news to their girl was a major problem.

Amy arrived at the pub they'd arranged to meet at and found Maya sitting at a quiet table, thumbing through the menu. Her daughter got up and gave her mother a big hug.

'Mum,' she said. 'I'm so glad to see you.'

'Me too,' replied Amy, sitting down and looking straight at Maya. They ordered some food and drink and settled down to talk. Amy took a deep breath – she didn't want to start their conversation off with the news about her and Dan. 'So, how are things at uni?'

Maya hesitated, wondering where she should start before replying. 'Well, the course work is very challenging. There is a whole load of reading to do from authors and dramatists in different centuries. And then lectures and seminars about the writers to attend and essays to write. All fascinating, Mum, but it's hard work. In fact today I need to finish off an essay about Thomas Hardy and rural England. Gripping stuff.'

'Oh no, I didn't realise' exclaimed Amy. 'I am so sorry. I am stopping you from working on your essay.'

'No, not at all. Seeing you is far more important. And I can tell you about James. Things are going really well between us. I think he's the one. But we've yet to take anything to the next level. I sometimes wonder if there is something holding him back.'

Amy looked surprised. All things seemed to be going so well the last time she had spoken to Maya about her love life.

'What's the problem?'

'Basically, I think he likes me. But he doesn't seem to want to take the initiative.'

'What exactly do you mean by that?' asked Amy.

'Well, when we go out together there are often hugs and kisses. That has been lovely, but then nothing else happens.'

'So what you mean is that you have not yet slept together. Are you ready for that, my love?' Amy asked in her usual blunt way.

'I think so, Mum,' Maya said, blushing. She had always been open with her mother but they had never discussed sex so openly. 'Although, honestly, there have been no opportunities to, I suppose. On our last date, he had to rush off home again to see to his mother again. Things are difficult for his parents. His mother is chronically ill and his father is a busy lawyer and so he's away often. They have a carer but she seems to have been ill recently and so James keeps being called back to the family home. It's just him. He has no brothers and sisters. So it's been nearly every weekend this month that he's had to go and spend time at home.' Maya sounded very resentful. 'Although, he has asked me to come to meet his parents at their big posh house to have supper with them. They apparently want to meet me.'

'Well, that's promising,' said Amy, brightly. 'So, what did you say?'

'I agreed to go, of course. When his mother is feeling up to it. But I'm worried. They have a real posh set up. I am not sure if my table manners are up to scratch… like knowing the way you should hold a soup spoon. Mum, what is the posh way of holding a soup spoon?'

'Absolutely no idea, my dear. By the handle?'

'Thank you, Mum. Very funny… ha ha!'

'I reckon that your James may be a little shy.'

Maya nodded her head vigorously in agreement, adding, 'Yeah, that really figures. James went to a boys' school so I get the impression he hasn't been around girls a lot.'

'That's very likely.'

'So, what am I supposed to do? How do I move things along?' asked Maya.

'If you really like him, give him more chances. Try things on with him. When he finally has free time, maybe at a weekend, take him back to your room. Maybe have a bottle of wine ready to open there so you both can relax together… and see how things go. It sounds like he really likes you. Just be *honest* how you feel about him. And, Maya, there is no rush. And you know that you must take precautions, right?' Amy was thinking about her own rushed relationship. She never regretted having Maya for a moment but she and Dan had been so young. She didn't want her daughter rushing into anything.

Maya blushed again, gave a big sigh and nodded thoughtfully.

'Has that helped?' asked Amy encouragingly.

'Yeah, I think so. Sort of,' replied Maya. 'Thank you, Mum. It's really good to be able to discuss these things. And how is Dad? And how are things with you guys. I couldn't help but notice things were tense before I left for uni. I am not even sure that I should be saying all this, but you and Dad did seem to have been having lots of arguments. It really does worry me. Sorry if I'm overstepping—'

'Let's finish eating first,' said Amy, looking down at her half-eaten pizza. 'Maybe then we could go over to Hampstead Heath and find a quiet place to talk more?'

'Oh. OK. No problem.' Maya looked puzzled at her mother's response and feared the worse.

Maya and Amy finished their meal. Amy paid and the two of them left the pub to walk across the Heath. Maya pointed to a wooden seat set back from the path.

'That looks good,' she said. 'A nice quiet spot. Just what we need.'

'It's fine with me,' said Amy. 'Let's sit down and I will tell you what's happening at home.'

Amy gathered her thoughts together as they sat down and she tried to figure out the best way to explain to her daughter what had happened.

'Listen to me. Your father and I have decided to separate. It's been a while coming. We've been arguing so much recently. We only seem to make each other so unhappy. So the only way forward for us both is to go our separate ways. I know it will hurt but it really is for the best.' Amy putting a comforting arm around Maya.

'I can't really believe this. Has he left you at the cottage? Is there someone else?' said Maya, who was now in tears.

'No. In fact, I am the one who has moved out. But yes, I have met someone. He is a lawyer and his name is Adam – we met through the Milchester Players group,' replied Amy.

'Oh my God! I thought something was going on with one of your drama friends,' exclaimed Maya. 'And you didn't tell me? How long has this been going on?'

'Look, Maya, it wasn't really the right time to tell you then. Remember, you had your exams and then all that business with Luke and then just about to start at uni.'

'OK, I take your point,' replied Maya, struggling to take it all in.

'Anyway,' continued Amy, 'I moved into Adam's flat in Milchester yesterday. We're living together now.'

'Bloody hell, Mum,' Maya paused, shocked. 'I knew you and Dad were having problems. I remember all the arguments, and you running upstairs in floods of tears to get away from the fighting. Oh my God, yes.'

'Yes, you've hit the nail on the head, Maya. There were many problems that we had to deal with. And it hasn't just been me moving on. I'm pretty sure your father has also had dalliances with other women.'

'Surely not!' exclaimed Maya.

'Yes. On that trip to Frankfurt, I phoned him in his hotel room in Germany, but he was in the shower. A woman picked up the call. I straightaway ended the call, as you can imagine.'

Maya did not reply.

'And that's not all,' replied Amy firmly. She suddenly felt the need to justify herself – she couldn't bear the idea of her daughter thinking she was the bad guy in this. 'The other thing is his drinking. It has been out of control for a while. The other night he just passed out on the sofa after too much wine.'

Maya again paused for thought. She eventually asked, 'So, is that everything? Is there anything else that I should know about?'

Amy paused and shook her head. 'I am so sorry to burden you with it. Me and your dad will still always be there for you. You're still our priority. But we just won't be together anymore.'

And so the two of them remained silently sitting on the bench, Amy's arm around Maya's shoulders.

Later, Amy went with Maya back to her room at Maynard College. After hugs and farewells, Amy headed back to Milchester and to Adam, feeling a certain element of relief. A difficult task had been executed. It had to be done, but she knew that it had very much hurt Maya. She thought briefly about letting Dan know that she had told Maya but then realised how difficult that conversation would be. Especially after she had asked him in the letter to hold off so they could do it together. She decided to wait and let the dust settle.

Chapter 15

The evening after Amy's visit, an exhausted Maya was lying on her bed, still thinking about what her mother had told her about the break-up of her parents' relationship. The revelations were still spinning around in her head, particularly his affair with another woman in Germany. Her mother must have been very annoyed about that. But how was her father dealing with the situation? Maya realised that she had only seen one side of the story. But when she had called the cottage, there was no answer again. She needed someone to talk to. She needed Anwen. She eyed a bottle of wine on her desk and wondered if her friend fancied a drink and a chat.

Inside she could hear Anwen was on the phone to someone. It sounded like a boy as she was giggling. Maya waited for a second more and heard Anwen end the conversation with a flirtatious sign off to her friend. She knocked at Anwen's door.

'Who is it?' Anwen sounded flustered.

'It's Maya. Fancy a drink? I've got some wine and I could do with a chat.'

Anwen appeared at the door, flushed and wearing just a nightie. Maya raised an eyebrow.

'Sorry,' Anwen grinned at her. 'Was on the phone to Simon.'

'Simon?' Maya smiled back at her.

'He's new,' Anwen said. 'I'm seeing him later tonight. Wine sounds good. Give me a second to get dressed.'

Maya smiled to herself. Simon was indeed new. A week ago it had been David. She retreated to her own room where she opened the wine. She realised that she wanted to talk to Anwen not only about what was happening with her parents, but she also wanted to ask her about what to do about James. She desperately wanted to find some way of igniting a fire in him. And Anwen seemed to be a good friend to ask for advice on that.

Anwen slid through Maya's door and gratefully accepted a mug of wine. Both the girls sat back on Maya's small single bed.

'Sorry about that,' Anwen said. 'He was telling me about what we're going to do later.' She laughed and took a sip of wine.

'You are trouble, Anwen,' Maya said, laughing too.

'What's happening with you?'

Maya took a deep breath. 'I had a long chat with my mum today. She came to London because she needed to tell me something. We had a real heart-to-heart.' Maya paused, looking awkwardly down at the floor. 'You don't mind me telling you all this family stuff, do you?'

'No, not at all. We're friends, Maya,' exclaimed Anwen.

'OK then,' said Maya. 'Well, first of all she told me that she and my dad have split up. In fact, she is now living with another man in Milchester. A lawyer apparently.' Maya was surprised to find herself welling up with tears. Anwen put her arm around her, comforting her.

'Oh no! What a shock. I am so sorry.' She paused and then added, 'You know it's not the end of the world though, right?'

'What?' Maya looked up at her.

'Sorry, I know you're upset,' Anwen said. 'But you'd said before that they argued *all* the time. And that they don't even sleep together. That's the end of a relationship for sure. My mum and dad split up five years ago. It was really hard at first but, once they both calmed down, it became easier. Me and my brother realised that we didn't have to take sides. And you know what…? Now they are both happier than ever. They're actually better friends than they ever were when they were living together. Should have split up sooner, if you ask me.'

Maya sighed. She hoped that Anwen was right and that her parents had made the right choice for them and for the entire family.

There was then a pause as the two girls wondered what to say next. Maya was the first to break the brief silence.

'What you said about sex and relationships…' she ventured.

'Yeeesss,' Anwen stretched the word out with relish.

'Well,' Maya continued. 'James and I are getting on so well. Really, really well. I was never ready before –

you know, to take things further – with other boyfriends. But I think I am now. I just can't figure out how to tell him, though. He's never even made a move other than to kiss me. I'm worried he's just not that interested in me. Please, please help me on this, Anwen. How do I get him to respond to me?'

Anwen smiled.

'Believe me. He likes you. You just need to give him a nudge in the right direction. I'll tell you how to seduce him. Just listen to this,' she said, bubbling with excitement. 'I assume that you are a good actress? Yes, of course you are!' Anwen proceeded to give Maya her best tips for engineering deeply romantic moments.

Maya's eyes grew larger and larger as she listened to the plan, punctuating Anwen's suggestions with loud comments.

'Oh my God! Yes! Yes! Brilliant!'

After five minutes or so Anwen had fired up Maya with a precise plan for how to show James she was ready for them to take the next step.

'Another wine?' suggested Maya.

'No, thanks,' replied Anwen, as she got up to go. 'I've done my duty here. And Simon awaits. Just be safe!' She bounded out of Maya's room, laughing.

It had been another long and testing day for Maya, but when she eventually went to bed she had a contented smile on her face. She now reckoned that she could deal with James, light the fire in him and get him going. What she felt for him was real and she was itching to take their relationship to the next level.

Just before she turned out her light, she messaged James and organised to meet him the following evening. Hopefully his mother's carer would be on duty at the house and they would not be interrupted this time.

****

The next evening the two not-quite-yet lovers met at the Woodsman pub. They drank wine and ate a meal. Maya thought about how comfortable she felt with James and hoped he felt the same way about being with her.

She eventually plucked up courage and asked him a question:

'You mentioned that girl you liked at school. Did you ever date her? I mean…Have you ever been in a serious relationship, James?'

James looked taken aback for a moment.

'I suppose not,' he answered. 'I've only ever wanted to date girls that I really felt a connection with so I haven't dated many.'

Maya smiled at the implication. 'You think we have a connection?'

'Yes,' James said, softly. 'Yes, Maya, I do.'

Maya had been thinking all along about Anwen's tips for getting her man but she suddenly remembered her mother saying that she should just be honest. The waiter came with the bill and James immediately insisted that he paid. Such a gentleman. She loved his good manners.

It was a chilly evening as they made their way through Highgate and beyond towards her uni and her room.

Maya had only worn a light coat and found herself

shivering in the late autumn air. James suddenly looked very concerned.

'You're cold. Here, just hold onto my arm and I'll wrap my coat around us both.'

Maya clutched his arm as closely as she possibly could until she could feel the warmth from James next to her. Then, somehow, she gathered the courage and pulled him to a quiet pathway, put her arms around him, pulling him closer and closer. She started to kiss him, hardly leaving him time to breathe. She eventually pulled away and looked into his eyes.

'Do you… do you want to come in when we get back to my room?' she asked, hardly daring to imagine what she would do if he said no.

'Are you sure?' James said, staring into her eyes.

'I am,' she said, firmly and again pulled him close to her, her hands moving slowly down over his body as they kissed. After a while she gently pulled herself away from him.

'Let's go now,' she said.

James nodded and Maya was elated. She could hardly believe this was happening. They were making their way back to her college. Nothing was said. Nothing needed to be said. They soon reached the building, climbed the stairs to Maya's floor and reached her door. She fumbled for her key and pushed open the door, her hands trembling. They were soon in a close embrace. Maya then started slowly unbuttoning his clothes.

But James suddenly stopped her and asked rather bashfully, 'Have you… you know… got protection?'

'Of course, you silly!' Maya smiled as she pulled a

drawer open to reveal that she was prepared. She then took off her own clothes and laid back on her bed, pulling him down to her. All was good and she was soon crying out for more.

Some while later, they were still lying together on the bed where they eventually fell asleep until morning. There were no phone calls from home. It was just the two of them.

In the morning, James kissed her awake and they made coffee. After showering, he told her he had a lecture at ten.

She then replied, in a soft, persuasive voice, 'I'm going to see you tonight, right?' He nodded.

After a final long and deep kiss Maya put on her robe and walked him to the main door of the building. She waved him goodbye and watched him walk purposefully away into the morning.

It had happened. James was her boyfriend now and she couldn't be happier.

Chapter 16

It was now late November. Amy had left Birch Cottage weeks ago for her new man. Dan had thrown himself into work and spent his nights – that had been getting longer and colder – alone and usually drinking. The cottage was haunted by silence. Dan even missed the tittle-tattle of Amy's voice as she had buzzed around the cottage like a demented wasp, complaining and telling him what to do and what not to do. Because she had now left him and was enjoying a new life in another man's bed.

The person Dan really missed was Maya. He had several messages from her on his phone but he had yet to find the strength to talk to her. Her messages were sweet – checking that he had enough to eat and was staying well. She had also told him that her new boyfriend, James, was lovely. Occasionally Dan put his head into her room which was now just collecting dust.

But there had come another blow for Dan. An email arrived late one Friday evening at work. It had been addressed to managers only and outlined an announcement from the German head office. UK sales had not been reaching the numbers they had strategised for when they branched out into the market. The parent company was going to be entering a period of consultancy on redundancies and would be meeting with the branch managers over the coming weeks.

The following week he was asked to attend a meeting at the UK head office in London on the Monday morning. He felt certain that the news couldn't be good. The only job that Dan had done since leaving university was ending. He was going to be made redundant after almost twenty years of service.

That night, he opened a bottle of Sicilian red. He mindlessly flicked through television channels as he finished it. Then he opened another bottle and was soon fast asleep on the sofa until the grandfather clock in the hallway struck one, waking him up from his snooze on the sofa. He felt angry with himself. He had fallen asleep on the sofa nearly every night that week. He knew, only too well, that he needed to stop drinking so much. He decided it was time to go to bed. He staggered uneasily to the open fire, tossed on some more logs to keep the room warm until morning and then stumbled up the stairs to his bedroom. He was soon fast asleep.

A couple of hours later he was woken by the sweet smell of wood smoke pouring into his bedroom and an odd hissing sound.

'What the hell?' he gasped, as he jumped out of bed and opened the door to see what was going on. The stairway and landing were full of dense smoke swirling upwards. He could hear flames roaring and crackling downstairs and he realised that he could already feel the heat from the fire on the floor beneath him. There was no way he could get down the stairs and so he quickly slammed the bedroom door shut and threw his duvet to the floor where he pressed it against the bottom of the door to stop the smoke from entering.

He turned and went to the window to try to get out onto the roof. He found the window was jammed shut so he smashed the glass letting in the night air, but he realised that he was going to be unable to get out. He had taken one of the spare rooms when he and Amy had stopped sharing a room. The window was small and positioned at the side of the cottage. He thought he could get through but the drop was sheer and he was sure he would break his legs.

Dan was now in a state of utter panic, and grabbed his phone to call 999. He was lucky, as he soon heard the siren of fire engines in the distance, getting louder and louder as they made their way up the winding road towards the cottage.

But the roaring of the fire downstairs had increased and more and more smoke was pouring under the bedroom door despite his efforts. Dan was coughing continuously. He was terrified and shaking.

He could now see the fire engine and the crew through the smashed bedroom window. He waved furiously. The next moments were a blur as the firefighters fought to control the flames downstairs. A ladder was placed at the side of the house and a fireman climbed up to assist Dan through the tiny window and down to the ground.

'Is there anyone else in the building?' one of the crew asked him as he checked Dan over.

'No.'

'We're glad we could get you out from the first floor. It would have taken us some time to get the fire under control and get upstairs to you. We've got an ambulance on the way to check you out. Is there anyone you can call?'

Dan thought for a moment, but was then overwhelmed by coughing again.

'Sit down here and rest until the paramedics get here. We've almost got the fire under control,' the fireman urged.

The ambulance arrived a few moments later and Dan let them check him over as he watched the firefighters work to extinguish the flames that had engulfed his home. The paramedics said that he was lucky and had got out before smoke inhalation could do any serious damage but that he should see his GP for a check-up in a few days just to be sure. They again asked if he had anyone he could call. This time Dan mumbled something about a friend. He had nobody to call but he couldn't quite admit that.

The fireman who had helped him out of the house returned to speak to him.

'I'm afraid your ground floor has been completely destroyed. It's not safe to be in there right now. It's probably salvageable but it will take a lot of work.'

'What happened?' Dan asked, feeling numb.

'We believe that the fire started in the sitting room,' the fireman said. 'There's no sign of any electrical cause. Do you use candles or other naked flames?'

Dan realised, in horror, that *he* had caused the fire. He

remembered drunkenly tossing logs onto the fire carelessly before bed and must have failed to put the fire guard in front of the log fire when he went upstairs. How much wine had he had? Too much he thought… His home was now destroyed and it was his fault. He wondered how he could live with all the devastation that he had caused. He was in a total mental mess.

Birch Cottage was a dark, smoking and yet somehow also dripping mess by the time the fire brigade finished some hours later. It was almost dawn. With a final reassurance that 'someone' was on the way, the emergency services left Dan standing in front of his ruined home. Of course, nobody was coming.

And so Dan spent a long hour sitting in his cold parked car, as he wondered where he could go from here. Eventually, Dan emerged bleary-eyed, cold and confused from his vehicle. He tottered over to the blackened remains of the cottage. The fire was out but the damage was devastating.

Dan could see the interior of the building through shattered windows and open doors on the ground floor. The grandfather clock in the hallway had crashed down to the ground and was a smoking black mass.

He thought about calling someone. Matt? Matt wouldn't answer his calls. Amy? Amy would be furious when she found out he'd destroyed their home. Maya? No, he couldn't face telling Maya what had happened to her bedroom. His father? Ollie was so sick, he couldn't bear the thought of calling him on the other side of the world to tell him what had happened. He realised that he had nobody to call. He was entirely alone.

Dan was feeling so bad – he could not cope with all that was happening in his world. It had been his fault that Sophie died. And, because of that, he had lost his twin brother. His relationship had ended in disaster. His home was destroyed and now he was being made redundant. He would have nothing left in his life. He felt desperate.

He started to walk through the woods, blinded by his despair. After an hour or so, it started to rain hard and eventually he was soaked. He turned round and retraced his muddy steps back to his car, cursing and feeling ever more desperate. Everything seemed to be against him.

Dan sat in the car and listened to the radio trying to somehow focus his mind and figure out what he should do now. But nothing changed. The sight of the ruins of the cottage completely sickened him.

He looked at his watch again. Somehow, it was now just after four o'clock in the afternoon. He had sat there all day. He decided to drive into Milchester. He had to get away from Birch Cottage – or what was left of it.

When he reached the city, he parked on the road next to the River Avon and sat in his car, thinking hard. The rain had stopped and it was now dark. The city was, by now, decked out with bright Christmas lights and passers-by were treated to the familiar sounds of carol singers and brass bands. But Dan hated it all. It all seemed so false. He needed to escape. He got out of the car and walked along the road next to the river, heading away from the bustle of the main road and towards a bridge.

At the bridge, he stopped and stared at the river

swirling and disappearing through the arches below him. It brought back to his mind, so vividly, the same dark water on that fatal day with little Sophie just six months ago. He remembered exactly what it had been like for him, swimming down to the bottom of that treacherous pond and pulling Sophie's body from the dark depths. But he had been too late. He had pulled her out but she had died. His brother's only daughter. And it had been all his fault, he thought. And that was why his brother couldn't forgive him. It had created this huge hole in his life where his brother – his twin – used to be. He had been drinking wine that day on the hill when he should have been alert and looking after Sophie. And then there was last night when the family home was consumed by fire. Everything was destroyed. And, of course, it was all his fault.

He thought about what had become of his relationship with Amy. They had loved each other at the beginning. He could never regret them bringing Maya into the world but their relationship had now completely fallen apart. What was he going to do now? Maya was growing up and she wouldn't need him the way she had done when she was a little girl. The job he had done since leaving university was now in danger of redundancy. And his home – the home they had brought up Maya in – was a burnt-up shell and that was his fault, too. He felt completely surplus to requirements. That seemed to sum up the situation right now. Dan suddenly felt desperate.

He felt nothing but despair at that very critical moment. His life had come to an end in so many ways. He suddenly became overwhelmed by an urge to climb up over the stone wall of the bridge and jump into the dark swirling water so that he could end it all. He hesitated and looked back at the lights of Milchester where he could just about still hear the distant sound of the brass bands. Then, he made his decision and started to clamber over the stone parapet of the bridge. But before he could go any further the phone in his pocket began to buzz.

He stopped, hesitated for a couple of seconds, and dropped back down onto the pavement. He pulled the phone out of his pocket.

Matt was calling him.

Chapter 17

Dan answered.

'Dan.' Matt sounded very worried. 'You OK?'

Dan was now making his way back to his car and could hardly believe what had happened.

'Matt, I'm so relieved to hear your voice. But things have been getting really bad in our immediate family. Amy has left me. And I think I might be made redundant soon. There was a fire at the cottage last night – a bad one. And so I've got nowhere to sleep at the moment. Well, would you believe I was just thinking about doing something very stupid with my life.'

'Oh my God, Dan, please tell me that you're OK now.'

'I think I'm OK now.' Dan paused.

'I don't know why, but I suddenly had the feeling that I needed to speak to you. Like a sharp pain in my head. I needed to call you. Remember that day you realised that I'd been knocked out in a rugby match at school? You somehow knew that I was hurt and begged Mum to get to me before the school could even get a call through. It was all very strange.'

'I do remember that day,' Dan said. 'I am so sorry, Matt. I really am in such a mess at the moment. Contact has been bad between us. I am so sorry for everything. Especially for Sophie.' Dan was now leaning against his car, trying to stop the tears coming to his eyes. He stood there, wondering what to do or say next.

'Look,' said Matt, 'I am just so very glad that you are OK. Listen, you're my *brother*. You've got to come here. But I'm not in Bristol anymore. I'm in London. Can you get to London? We can work things out.'

'Yes, good idea,' replied Dan, feeling an overwhelming sense of relief that he and Matt were now on speaking terms again. 'It's been so good to speak to you again after such a long time. I think I'll find a B&B to stay in tonight. I'll need to contact the insurance company and speak to the police about the fire. But I have a meeting with work in the London head office and so I'll head down on Monday. Text me your address.'

'You are sure you're OK? And OK to look after yourself until then?' Matt said.

'I am now,' Dan answered. 'Thank you. I will see you soon.'

The call ended.

Dan drove off in his car, leaving behind him the bright and cheerful Christmas decorations and jolly brass bands. He entered the dark night of the Cotswold countryside again. Out of habit, he drove straight back to Birch Cottage.

'Damn it!' he cursed as he stared at the ruins of his home, still smoking. He turned the car around, wheels spinning, and headed off down to the village. It was now very dark as he pulled up at the local Kings Arms pub which he knew had rooms. He signed up for two nights and was soon sitting down to a welcome hot meal.

Later, sitting in his bedroom chair, he thought about what had almost happened and what had happened. In that moment, he had really been certain about jumping and, if Matt hadn't called, he would probably be in that dark water by now. But Matt *had* called. Something had made Matt call him. He didn't care if it was luck or their psychic link. He had his brother back in his life.

****

The next day Dan spent time sorting out the insurance company and speaking with the police about the fire. They confirmed that they would be treating the fire as accidental. He wouldn't be able to live at the cottage for months – maybe even years.

On Sunday, he slept most of the morning and in the evening decided to call Matt again. He needed to talk.

'Dan,' his brother said, 'Are you OK?'

'I'm OK,' replied Dan. 'I'm still coming to London tomorrow.'

'Great. But how about chatting now? I have plenty of time this evening. What happened with Amy?'

Dan hesitated, and then told his brother how his relationship had ended.

'Well… it's a long story. I suppose I did see it coming,' said Dan. 'We'd been drifting apart for years. In fact we haven't shared a bed in ages. We live practically separate lives. Amy had started flirting with other men. I even slept with a work colleague in Frankfurt and she found out but didn't seem to care. In fact she had started having a serious affair with a sleazy lawyer she had met in her local amateur dramatics group. Then Maya left for university. And everything just fell apart after that.' Dan paused. He was getting very emotional. 'Amy left me in October and moved into a smart flat in Milchester. And so it has been a bloody awful time for me, I can tell you.'

'Oh no!' exclaimed Matt. 'You certainly have been through it.'

'Added to all that is that I'm likely to get made redundant tomorrow, and now the cottage is burnt down. I'm sure you get the full picture.'

'And what about Maya?'

'She's absolutely fine. She's loving university life and has a new boyfriend. I am just so grateful she wasn't in the house when it caught fire. I could never have forgiven myself...' Dan trailed off. The death of Matt's daughter hung in the air between them.

'You seem to have had a rough time of it,' Matt said calmly. 'Well, it's like this... I've moved to London, like I said, and I have a spare room in my flat. Come and stay with me. I'm in Camden.'

Dan was lost for words.

'Are you still there?' asked Matt anxiously.

'Yes, yes... of course. I am trying to take all this in. I am so grateful to you and, if I come to London, I can be nearer to Maya. You are so kind. It all sounds like a great idea. Would Lisa be OK with me staying, asked Dan?'

Matt did not reply immediately.

'Matt? Hello? What's wrong? Is Lisa OK?'

Matt eventually answered, choosing his words carefully. 'She's fine. I am not sure if I want to talk about this over the phone. But things are a bit complicated with Lisa. Perhaps we should wait until you come up to London? We can talk about it then.'

'OK, that sounds fine to me,' replied Dan, wondering what could have happened.

The conversation ended, Dan was both surprised and delighted to have made contact with his brother again, but he was concerned about Matt's answer regarding Lisa. He sensed that there was something that Matt was keeping to himself. Time would tell, he thought.

Chapter 18

Monday arrived. It was the day that Dan was leaving to go and stay with his brother and also the day of the meeting at the London head office that would decide the future of his career. He left his car in the long-stay car park at Milchester station and was soon sitting in the quiet carriage feeling nervous about what would come from this meeting. If he was made redundant it would mean no regular income for him and a complete change in his life. It really was the end of an era for him.

Dan was definitely in a mental mess, but seeing Matt was something to look forward to. His thoughts came to a halt as the train pulled into London Paddington station, before disgorging crowds of commuters onto the platform. Dan joined the scramble for the Underground.

The meeting was with a man Dan had never heard of, Jack Elderton. Dan arrived early at the south London UK head office of Leichmatic and was given coffee in reception. The offices looked sparsely decorated as if the company wasn't planning on staying much longer. There was no artwork on the wall as there had been when he visited before. It reminded him of his previous meeting with Herr Schneider in Frankfurt when he had been told about the threat a failing UK market would cause for a company that wanted to achieve a successful merger. He'd been worried about this day coming ever since that meeting.

After a long wait, an officious-looking woman appeared at the door.

'Good morning, Mr Barnes. Yes, Mr Elderton will see you now. Follow me, please.'

Dan was shown into an impressively smart room overlooking the River Thames. Mr Elderton, a serious-looking man, stepped forward and shook Dan's sweaty hand.

'Good morning, Mr Barnes. Please do sit down. My name is Jack Elderton and, as you probably know, I have been appointed by Leichmatic Deutschland to wrap up business interests here in the UK.'

Dan sat down, attempting a feeble smile. Mr Elderton also sat and continued. He looked uncomfortable as he glanced down over his desk, flicking through his paperwork.

'Ah yes, of course, I see you live near Milchester. A lovely part of the world, isn't it?' Dan wished that Mr Elderton would stop the sweet talk and come to the point. 'May I call you Daniel?'

'Yes, fine. No problem,' replied Dan, still wondering why the hell the manager was still dithering around so much.

'And so, Daniel,' Mr Elderton continued, tapping his finger nails on his desk, 'I am afraid that the

German office has decided to cease trading in the UK. Sales have not been buoyant enough to support the running of the business. I am afraid that the lease on your branch premises in Milchester, along with other regional offices will not be renewed next month. The London office will handle all outstanding client orders before finally closing in the spring of next year. Leichmatic may be able to revisit the UK market at a later date but I am afraid it just isn't working right now.'

Dan said nothing. He looked past and out of the window where the sun was shining down on the River Thames flowing. He knew exactly what was coming next from Mr Elderton.

'I'm very sorry, Daniel. I know this will come as a blow for you and your team, who will all be informed in due course. I know you have served this company for very many years—'

'Twenty years, actually.' Dan was beginning to get irritated by Mr Elderton.

'Errr... yes, that's right' replied Mr Elderton, checking the paperwork in front of him. 'We will, of course, being making you a generous redundancy package which I hope will help you move on with your career.' Mr Elderton paused. 'Do you have any more questions, Daniel? For instance, would you like to make an appointment with one of the company's senior managers to discuss any questions that you have?'

Dan, feeling very angry, attempted to collect his thoughts and remain calm. He coughed loudly and answered, trying not to sound too sarcastic.

'I don't think so, Mr Elderton. I think I get the message. I will be taking immediate leave for the rest of the year and I look forward to hearing what my redundancy package involves. And thanks for your very precious time.'

Dan got up from his chair, ignored Mr Elderton's offered handshake and strode out of the room, banging the door behind him. As soon as he left the building, he phoned Matt.

'So, how did it go?' asked Matt anxiously. 'Tell me all. Is it bad news?'

'It was a total fucking disaster,' replied Dan pausing for breath. 'But can we talk about it later when I see you? I'm on my way. You said Camden Town, didn't you?'

'Yes… see you there soon,' replied Matt, rather worried about his brother.

****

An hour later, Matt met Dan at the entrance to Camden Town station. They hesitated, not knowing at first what to say or to do, before they then joined together in a big hug.

'We can walk to my place from here,' suggested Matt. 'We can go along by the canal which runs right past my flat. It is very scenic and I think you will like it.' Matt paused. 'And then we can talk about your interview?'

'Yes, OK,' replied Dan, not sure that he really wanted to.

And so the twin brothers set off along the canal towpath, chatting away. As they walked along, Dan gave Matt a blow-by-blow account of all that had happened in the meeting with Mr Elderton. Matt listened to him carefully. He realised that his brother was definitely not in a good way.

They soon reached the block where Matt had a flat overlooking the canal. Matt took Dan to see the spare bedroom. It had a balcony with views of the canal. Dan hadn't brought much with him as so much had been smoke-damaged in the fire but he unpacked his rucksack with a variety of shirts, underwear, toiletries and other bits and pieces.

Matt then took Dan into the sitting room and left him on the sofa to look through two big scenic windows which had a wide view over the canal. Dan was, at last, beginning to cool down after his interview. Matt returned from the kitchen with bottles of beer and a big smile on his face.

Dan hesitated. 'Matt,' he said, faltering. He realised that he hadn't had a drink since the fire. It was the longest he had been without alcohol for a good while. 'Matt, have you got something soft?

'It's OK,' Matt smiled. 'These are alcohol-free. Let's talk about what has happened with clear heads.'

Dan smiled at his brother, grateful for the understanding.

'So, Dan,' said Matt, 'you sure have had a rough time recently.'

Dan heaved a big sigh. 'I really don't know where to start. The cottage is in a real mess. The ground floor is burnt out completely and the upstairs is damaged by the water from the fire brigade. Fortunately the roof is intact. But at the moment I really don't feel that I want to go back, even if everything is replaced.'

'Yeah, yeah, I do understand,' answered Matt. 'I

can well believe you there. It must have been horrific.'

'Of course,' replied Dan, 'I called Dad to tell him before I left Milchester. And he is dealing with the insurance company from Australia. He's actually coping really well with his Parkinson's Disease. I'm just glad he wasn't angry with me about the fire.'

'He called me after he spoke to you. He's just glad you're OK. You can stay here as long as you need. And I'm guessing Milchester isn't a great place to look for work right now?' asked Matt, changing the subject.

Dan pulled a face and replied, 'No. Maybe a career change might be easier here in the city. I really think I have had enough of kitchens, taps, fridges, freezers and ovens... and so on. God knows what I'll do though. But it will be good to be nearer to Maya. I haven't spoken to her for a while and I need to tell her what has really has been going on between me and Amy. I am sure that woman has been poisoning my name. Yes, I think that would be a really good move. Thanks, Matt. You've really saved my life.'

'You're my brother,' Matt said. 'Whatever happens, you're always my brother.'

'Matt, I hope I am not treading on a sensitive area here, but what has happened with you and Lisa? Where is she?' Dan had seen no sign of Lisa in the small flat. In fact, it looked like Matt was living alone.

Matt sighed. 'Yeah. I suppose it's my turn now. Lisa and I have had a lot of problems since Sophie... Well, in fact we're not living together anymore. We've separated.'

'Oh no, I am so very sorry,' said Dan. He felt lost

for words. All he could think of was that terrible accident in the pool on the picnic. He had visions in his mind's eye of Matt and Lisa's only child, Sophie, sinking down as he attempted to rescue her from the dreadful, deep, dark pool on Woodbury Hill.

Matt spoke slowly and shook his head. 'We tried so hard to have Sophie. When Lisa got pregnant it felt like a miracle. We then tried to get pregnant again after Sophie was born. We'd tried for five whole years to have another baby. When we lost her we were in the middle of tests to find out if there were any problems.'

'Oh, Matt, I had no idea,' Dan murmured.

'After a bunch of tests, they confirmed that the problem was in fact me. My sperm count is low. Very low. They're not sure how we managed to have Sophie. She really was a miracle.'

'Do they know why? Is there anything they can do to improve your chances?'

Matt was getting worked up and was visibly upset and struggling to continue.

'No. They said these things just happen. We could have tried IVF. We were thinking about it but then Sophie…'

Dan stayed quiet. He couldn't imagine the pain Matt still felt over losing his daughter.

'Anyway, neither of us could deal with the grief. In fact Lisa and I started having really serious arguments. She said she wanted to try IVF immediately and maybe even a sperm donor. I couldn't even contemplate it whilst we were so raw from losing Sophie. She got angry with me and said I was wasting time.' Matt paused to get his breath back and Dan put his hand on Matt's arm, a gesture of support and understanding. 'And we just kept fighting. In fact, everything between us just fell apart and that's when we decided to separate.'

'Bloody hell, Matt!' exclaimed Dan 'I had no idea about all this. I am so sorry...' Dan then paused. 'Where is Lisa living?'

'Believe it or not, she's moved to Australia for a year,' replied Matt. 'Maybe she had to go to the other side of the world from me and from the memories. And I didn't want to stay in Bristol so I changed jobs and moved here in London. So, it's a new start for me, too. I still love her so much but I don't think we can ever make it work now. Sophie's loss – it was just too much for either of us.'

The brothers now became quiet and thoughtful.

'Matt,' Dan was speaking quietly and thoughtfully. 'I know you blame me for Sophie. For what happened to her. I want you to know that I blame myself, too. I am so very sorry, I—'

'Dan,' Matt said, suddenly. 'Please listen to me. I really don't blame you so much now. I did at first, but not now. It was a horrible, tragic accident. I know that you did everything you could and that you would never do anything to hurt Sophie or Lisa or me.' Matt looked at his brother. They both had tears in their eyes.

'I just feel so guilty,' Dan said. 'I feel like I am a terrible man... everything I touch turns to shit.'

'You are a *good* man,' Matt said. 'Because you are *my* brother.' Dan smiled and the two of them embraced.

'Anyway. We need to get some rest now,' Matt

announced. 'Tomorrow we begin our futures. And what you really need is a new job, and this new home – closer to Maya... And isn't there something very important you haven't yet mentioned that is missing in your life?' His face broke out in a big smile. Dan looked quizzical. 'How about a new woman in your life?'

Matt could always read his brother's mind. Dan had always been in a relationship. Things hadn't been good with Amy for a while now and he sorely missed the love of a woman.

'Correct! That's it, Matt, in a nutshell. I'd love to meet a new woman.'

'Well, I'm not sure about finding your next big love right away, but I will do my very best,' Matt chuckled and then put on a serious face. 'And I can help with another thing. You can live here with me.'

'You are so kind,' said Dan, 'I really don't deserve it.'

'Don't be silly' replied Matt. 'After all, we are brothers and twin brothers, too.'

'I think I need some sleep,' said Dan.

'Come with me then,' replied Matt, 'I will show you to your room.'

The two brothers stood up and had a long and meaningful hug before Dan headed off to the spare bedroom. All was well between them.

After Dan had settled down in his new bed he lay awake for a while, thinking about how tragic events had driven him and his twin brother apart but had also brought them back together again. He thought about what Matt had said about him being a good man and wondered if he would ever feel that that could, in fact, be true.

Chapter 19

Dan settled into the flat and life with his twin brother over the next few days. The rift between the two of them was gradually healing and they were, once again, finding the close connection they had shared since their birth. It would all take time and Dan still sometimes felt as if he was walking on hot coals.

He had spoken briefly to Maya and explained that he was now living with Uncle Matt in London. Maya was delighted to hear that her father was much closer and had been very sympathetic about the fire at the cottage. Dan asked her briefly about what her plans were for Christmas and she said that she would be happy to meet up with the family. She also promised Dan that they would most definitely see each other soon.

Dan had also contacted Amy about what had happened at Birch Cottage. She was very upset about the memories they had inevitably lost – baby pictures and trinkets – but she was genuinely relieved that he was not hurt and was now staying with Matt.

Meanwhile, on the Sunday morning, Matt came into Dan's bedroom and found him staring out of the window, watching with great interest a young woman with dark hair walking on the other side of the canal and carrying a bulky bag of shopping.

'Talent spotting again?' asked Matt cheekily.

'Yeah,' replied Dan wearily. 'Just having a break from looking for suitable job vacancies in sales. But no luck so far. Maybe the new year will see a few more positions come up.'

Dan walked to his bed, closed his laptop and yawned loudly. Matt could see that his brother needed some light relief.

'You know something,' commented Matt, 'You might be interested to hear that I know that woman you were watching. She lives in a flat not far from here.' Matt paused. 'Actually, Dan, we know each other rather well.'

Dan gave Matt a furtive smile and asked him a question.

'So you are rather more than just good friends? I had no idea you were seeing someone.'

'Well, yes,' replied Matt. 'If you must know, her name is Maria and we have been seeing each other for about a month. She works in an Italian restaurant owned by her family which was where we got to know each other. Her parents came to the UK before she was born. She sometimes drops in here to see me for a coffee when she finishes work.'

'Oh yes?' said Dan, smirking. 'Just a cuppa is it? Is that all? I think I get the picture, Matt.'

'Yes, but it's really complicated. She's married,' replied Matt. 'She is hitched up to an Italian. His name is Francesco, a real brute of a man. He imports Italian wine. And regularly drinks it. A lot of it.'

'And does this husband have any idea about what's going on between you two?'

'I don't think so. I certainly hope not. Maria and I have been so careful. Being Italian, family and family loyalty are very important to her but also her marriage isn't happy. She told me that she had wanted to go to college to study history – she's really very intelligent. But her parents had other ideas for her future. They thought she should get married. When she met Francesco she was very young – just eighteen. He was very good-looking back then but not so much now.

'If she was ever happy with him, she certainly isn't now. She told me that Francesco has a terrible temper on him. In fact, he sounds like he is a real beast when he gets going. I know all this because she says she needs someone like me to talk to. It is really awful the way he behaves. Maria tells me that he is often rough with her in bed. Sometimes he slaps her. If he is in the kitchen and gets really angry he throws plates and smashes them on the floor. She would leave him but she's frightened of what he will do. In fact…' here Matt paused, before continuing, 'if he found out about me I honestly think he'd kill her and then me.'

'Bloody hell, Matt, I hope you know what you're doing,' exclaimed Dan. 'Can't you help her get away from him? It sounds like an abusive marriage.'

'It is,' replied Matt. 'It breaks me every time she leaves to go back there. I've told her she can stay with me. But she's so frightened of what he will do. We have to be careful for now and figure out how she can get away from him safely. I don't want to rush her but equally I am terrified of what he might do to hurt her. We are really very fond of each other. I haven't felt this way about anyone since Lisa. I've told Maria all about this year – my marriage breaking down and Sophie…'

There was a silence as the brothers remained watching Maria make her way down the path and into the distance along the canal.

But suddenly Dan pointed out to Matt another attractive young woman walking briskly along the towpath. She had tied up her dark hair, wore a nurse's uniform, and was obviously in a hurry. She entered the block of flats on the other side of the canal.

'Oh my God,' exclaimed Dan. 'She is a real beauty.'

'Ah, well you'll be pleased to learn that I also know that woman,' said Matt. 'Her name is Cristina and she comes from Romania… Bucharest, I believe. She has one of the ground floor flats in that block. She works in the local hospital.'

'Yes,' said Dan. 'Good so far… How do you know her?'

Matt continued, 'She is one of the regulars at the King James pub. I sometimes chat with her. I occasionally see her there with a guy who may well be Romanian, too. But I am not at all sure there. They always seem to chat away in some foreign lingo. There doesn't seem to be much affection between them so I have no idea whether he's her boyfriend. It's all very intriguing.'

Dan remained silent, his mind was suddenly fixated on Cristina.

****

Christmas was around the corner and Dan had kept looking out for Cristina as well as for promising job adverts. But he had not yet caught sight of her again. He had also been with Matt to the King James pub – for soft drinks only, of course – but there had been no sign of her there either.

Dan was really keen be introduced to Cristina and Matt was very aware of his brother's situation. And he assured him that he would do his best to engineer a meeting soon. He reckoned that Christmas would be a good time. This little community in north London put on and enjoyed lots of social events around the holiday.

As Christmas neared, Maya made her decision about where she would spend Christmas. She called Dan to let him know.

'Dad, I've decided the best thing is to spend Christmas day with Laura and her family in Milchester. Mum says she and Adam are going to Paris for the holiday and they invited me with them but it feels weird. I don't really know him yet. And I'd miss you too much. So I'm going to stay with Laura. And the day after Boxing Day, James's parents have invited me to stay and meet his entire family.'

'That sounds lovely,' Dan said. He felt a sudden pang but he understood that it would be hard for her to choose between her two parents for the first time this year.

'So, you and Uncle Matt will be together, right? You won't be on your own? I couldn't bear that.'

'We will be fine,' Dan assured her.

'Love you, Dad,' she signed off.

Dan was still very sad that this would be the first day he would see Christmas Day without his little girl. But he suddenly realised that it would be Matt's first Christmas without his little girl, too. He began to sense the dark shadow of depression coming down over him again. He had not found any good jobs to apply for so far, and he had not seen Cristina. There were nights that he considered reaching for a bottle of wine again but he knew he couldn't go back there.

There then came a moment of Christmas joy. He received a card from Maya with a comic Santa Claus picture and a message which touched his heart.

> *'Dear Dad,*
> *I want to wish you a very merry Christmas. I will miss seeing you so much. I so much remember all our Christmases – the tree, the mistletoe, and you putting flour in your beard and pretending to be Father Christmas. You did make me giggle! And all that scrummy food and the drink. So many happy memories.*
> *I do hope I can see you in the new year. The sooner the better!*
> *Lots of love from Maya xx.'*

Dan read the card a number of times. He welled up, desperately wanting to see his daughter again. Dan also received a Christmas greeting of sorts from Amy via a text message.

> 'Please keep an eye on Maya while we are away in Paris and call me if there are any problems. Merry Christmas.'

'Hmmm. Typical Amy. Bossy boots,' Dan muttered, shaking his head. Amy had always had a habit of making him very angry, and also very sad.

In addition to these messages, Dan had just received

the long awaited official confirmation of his redundancy package from Leichmatic. It was generous but it was still his worst Christmas present ever. He still felt the sting of being unwanted and discarded. And once his payment ran out, he would need a steady income. He very much wanted to build a new future. Maybe buy his own place – somewhere that Maya could come and visit and bring her boyfriend. He needed a new job to make that happen.

He was looking through job adverts when Matt joined him in the lounge just a few days before Christmas.

'How's it going?'

'You know… there just doesn't seem to be any kitchen design companies hiring in the city at the moment.'

Matt tried his best to reassure and help his brother. 'There will be more in the new year. Anyway, let me have a look for you. I wondered whether you have considered another line in sales, you know… selling a different type of product. I would have thought you have the skills for all sorts of things.'

'That's not a bad idea.' Dan passed his laptop to Matt who started to scan through the pages and pages of sales positions. Then he suddenly became excited.

'Hey, Dan, how about this one? Just up your street! Get into property sales. They're looking for new estate agents. The market here in London is booming. You'd be really good at it. Look. This is Ellington and Davies and they are currently expanding operations and looking for experienced salespeople for a branch around the corner covering the whole of north London. They provide you with a car so you could sell the Land Rover you've got parked in Milchester. Make a fresh new start.' Matt was grinning at his brother as he spoke.

Matt passed the laptop back to Dan.

'Thanks Matt. This sounds like a winner. I will get on with an application right now.'

Later in the day Dan bounced back into the kitchen, full of himself. He had sent off an application to the estate agent and he hoped that they would contact him in the new year. It would indeed be a new start.

****

Christmas Day passed by quietly for Dan and Matt, who stayed at the flat eating and watching the traditional Christmas TV shows and movies. Later in the evening, Dan was woken from a doze on the sofa by his phone ringing. It was Maya.

'Hi Dad. Merry Christmas! Just thought I would give you a call today and see how you and Uncle Matt were getting on. Have you had a good day?'

Dan sat up in his chair. 'It is so good to hear you,' he said. 'All is fine here, except of course, I haven't been able to see you. I miss you, Maya. So what have you been up to today?'

'Well… as I am staying with Laura's family, I have been on my best behaviour.'

'Oh yes, of course you have.'

'But tomorrow I am meeting James's parents and I am *so* nervous.'

'Why?' Dan sounded confused.

'Well, his family is so posh that I am shitting my

pants at the thought of going to see them. Do you have any tips?'

'Errr… just let me think.' Dan thought. 'I think you should just be polite. And don't drink too much. And all you really need is to be your naturally lovely self.'

'Thanks so much, Dad…' Maya paused. Dan could hear voices in the background.

'Laura's come to let me know dinner is ready, Dad. I will have to sign off now. Happy Christmas… Love you to bits. And love to Uncle Matt. And I will see you soon.'

The line went dead. But Dan was on cloud nine. The sound of his daughter's voice saying 'Happy Christmas… Love you to bits,' brought a lump in his throat.

****

On Boxing Day morning, Dan suggested to Matt over breakfast that after such a quiet Christmas they really should be out and about to celebrate New Year's Eve.

'How about the traditional New Year's Eve celebration meal and party at the King James?' suggested Matt. 'They still have places and I am sure it will be excellent.'

'Yeah. Good plan,' replied Dan.

Matt continued, 'And then we could take a wander up to the nearby Frederick Park to watch the midnight firework displays over north London. They are amazing, apparently. I'll head to the pub and book our tickets today.'

'Let's do it,' replied Dan.

'The perfect night out. Good food and…' Matt

winked at his brother.

'And what? Spit it out, Matt.'

'Good company, of course. Loads of people will be there. I expect Cristina will be there, if she isn't working.'

'I'm definitely there. Count me in!' exclaimed Dan.

London was really beginning to tick all the boxes.

****

And so, on New Year's Eve, Matt and Dan walked down the canal towpath towards the King James pub. The dark sky was already punctuated by whistling and exploding rockets even though it was still early. They reached the pub and found a table next to the window where they could watch all the comings and goings. Dan noted that Maria was sitting with a group of friends and noisily chatting away. Dan saw her eyes flick daringly up to catch Matt's. He nudged Matt who silently nodded. He had clearly not expected to see her there tonight.

'The man on her left is her husband,' Matt said, quietly. The man looked heavy-set and dark-haired. Dan felt sorry for his brother that he couldn't be with the woman he cared so much for on New Year's Eve.

As they were deciding on what to eat, the door to the pub swung open. A woman with dark hair walked towards the bar. Dan followed her back with his eyes. She was on her own and looked around the pub as if trying to find someone. Possibly a date. She waited, looking at her watch.

When she turned around to scan the pub, Dan saw that it was Cristina. She was wearing a stunning and very low-cut dress and looked beautiful. At long last, they were in the same place. He must find a way to speak to her. But how? Things could be awkward if she was on a date with someone else.

But he did not need to worry about a date because Francesco stood up and called her over to where his party was sitting. Cristina smiled and she sidled over to Francesco's table. They must know each other, Dan thought. Francesco introduced her to his friends at his table as 'Cristina, the beauty from Bucharest'. Which was exactly what she was, with her glossy black hair, olive skin, and dark eyes. Cristina and Maria greeted each other with a kiss on each cheek. Dan wondered if their friendship was why Cristina had been invited. She couldn't possibly like a man like Francesco.

During their meal, Dan stole glances at Cristina, but she was so involved in conversation with Maria that she did not notice him. But as the evening progressed she finally noticed this dark-haired, bearded man glancing at her. She locked eyes and returned Dan's glance with a shy smile. Dan noted that Matt and Maria avoided any eye contact throughout the meal and, again, he felt sorry for his brother.

At the end of the meal, Dan and Matt found themselves walking behind Francesco's party of friends up the hill to Frederick Park. They had clearly had the same idea as Matt about watching the fireworks.

As they stood in the icy night air, waiting for the fireworks, Dan noticed that Cristina had moved away from the group of friends and was standing with another group who she seemed to know well, too. He nudged his brother and nodded in her direction. Matt smiled and worked his magic by introducing Dan and

Cristina to each other. They were both naturally shy but the noise of the rockets exploding and the sight of bright flashing over the city was absolutely stunning and captivated them. They were soon chatting away about her work at the hospital, Dan's job hunt and where they both found themselves.

Midnight arrived dramatically. There was a mighty climax of rockets exploding, sparkling and falling over the London skyline. After the fireworks were over, the gathering slowly turned to each other, talking and laughing together as they started to walk back down the hill.

One of the group Cristina was with called out to her. 'Come on Cristina. We have drinks to go to. Leave the poor man alone.'

'I am so sorry, Dan. I have to go now. We're heading back to Maria and Francesco's for more drinks,' she said with a note of regret in her voice. 'It was really nice meeting you.'

'I'd like to see you again' said Dan to Cristina. 'Could I perhaps call you?'

'OK,' she said, handing him her phone. 'How about this? Just key in your number and I'll call you.'

As Dan tapped in his number she gave him a meaningful smile. He handed it back and she said goodbye before she disappeared down the hill with her Italian neighbours and Dan's number.

'Time for bed, Dan?' Matt asked, grinning knowingly. 'Looks like you have made a good impression on her.'

'I really hope so,' exclaimed Dan.

Cristina had his telephone number. The waiting game had begun.

Chapter 20

Dan and Matt were lounging on the sofa in their flat after returning home, taking stock of what had happened at the dramatic fireworks display when Dan had finally met Cristina.

'I can't believe it has actually happened,' exclaimed Dan, shaking his head. 'And that she's got my number.'

'I hope it works out for you. She's a real beauty.'

'Do you think that guy you mentioned that you'd seen her with is her boyfriend?'

'No idea. They definitely speak the same language so maybe he's family.'

'Ah yes,' replied Dan. 'He might be a relation or family friend. Do they act like they are a couple?'

'Oh, Dan,' replied Matt. 'I wouldn't worry. Why would she have taken your number if she had a boyfriend?'

'You're right,' Dan said. 'Here's to the new year and a new start.' They raised and clinked their glasses of coke. Within ten minutes the two brothers had gone to their respective beds, and Dan was sound asleep and dreaming of Cristina.

****

The first morning of the new year duly arrived, and a dazed Dan was sitting in the kitchen. He grabbed a quick bowl of muesli and wondered when Cristina might get in touch. But he need not have worried, for when he returned to his room and picked up his phone there was already a message flashing on the screen. It had been delivered half an hour ago.

> 'It was great to meet you last night. I'd love to meet up for a meal or a drink or something. Cristina xx.'

There was no time like the present he told himself as he picked up his phone. He called her. There was no reply and he decided not to leave her a message just yet. Perhaps she would call him back soon.

When he still hadn't heard from Cristina again, he called her phone in the late afternoon. There was again no reply, but this time Dan decided to leave a brief message:

'Hi Cristina, this is Dan. Thanks for your message. I so much enjoyed meeting you and I too hope that we might be able to meet up again soon. Give me a call sometime.'

****

Dan discussed Cristina with Matt over supper that evening. Matt soon became concerned that Dan was getting obsessed by this Romanian beauty and so he decided to give him some brotherly advice.

'You know, Dan, you don't want her to think you're too keen. It's only been a day. She might be tied up at work and hasn't had time to get in touch. She fancies you... obviously... because she said in the message that she'd like to meet up. But you must not frighten the pants off the poor girl.'

Dan shook his head and swiftly changed the subject, 'Anything good on to watch tonight? I need something gripping to occupy my mind.'

They decamped into the sitting room and chose a sci-fi movie about a world invasion by aliens. Dan, as expected, was soon fast asleep on the sofa. But not for long. His mobile started to buzz. It was Cristina. He woke up, jumped up and rushed into the kitchen to take the call. She sounded rather nervous and formal, but he loved her voice and her accent.

'Hello, this is Cristina. Am I speaking to Dan?'

'Yes. Hi. I'm so glad you called back.'

Cristina hesitated. 'Yes, I am sorry I took a while to get back to you. I have been working a very tiring shift at the hospital. It has been a very difficult time. But it is very good to speak to you now.'

'And you too,' replied Dan. He paused and then made his move. 'Cristina, I was wondering if you would like to meet up for a drink sometime?'

'That would be lovely,' replied Cristina. 'How about tomorrow? My shift finishes earlier, so I can be free at...' she paused, working out her schedule, '8.30. Is that OK for you?'

'That's fine with me,' replied Dan

'So, let's meet at the Wheatsheaf pub,' suggested Cristina. 'It's only a short walk further than the King James and it looks over the canal. It is more... how do you say it in English? It is more private than the King James.'

'It sounds good to me.' Dan silently agreed with her choice. He didn't want to run into Francesco while he was on a date with her. 'So I look forward to seeing you then.'

He slowly made his way into the sitting room where the movie was reaching its crazy climax. The world would be saved. He looked down at Matt who was sitting on the edge of the sofa, glued to the TV.

'Well, Matt, that was Cristina. We have a date for tomorrow.'

'That's great,' Matt said, smiling. 'You'd better get your beauty sleep then.' Dan yawned and turned to leave the room.

'Lucky Dan,' muttered Matt as his brother left.

Dan got into bed, his brain spinning with flashbacks of meeting Cristina. It took him a long time to get to sleep, wondering about what might happen the following day.

****

Conversation between the brothers over breakfast on the following morning was limited. Dan had much on his mind. Matt headed back into work but it was a day at home for Dan, sitting in his room online with his laptop and waiting for news of a job interview.

But he just could not concentrate. He kept looking through the window at the canal footpath. There had been a frost overnight but now the sun was reflecting up from the canal. Maybe he would see Cristina in her nurse's uniform on the footpath on her way to the shops or to work? After a lunch of a cheese sandwich he decided to take some fresh air by pacing along the canal footpath. He found the Wheatsheaf pub at which they were meeting later and then returned to the flat. He needed to get himself ready for the date.

The night inevitably closed in and darkness crept over the canal. As 8.30 approached, Dan set off briskly for his date. It was bitterly cold outside and the moon was now high in the sky. He soon reached the pub and, through the window, caught sight of the dark-haired Cristina sitting at the bar. She was wearing a dark blue jacket which she had partly unbuttoned to reveal a striking red dress. She saw him enter and gave him a wave as he approached her. She hadn't yet ordered a drink.

'Hi,' she said, welcoming him with a big smile.

'Hi,' he replied. 'Let's find a table. A little corner somewhere, maybe?'

'That will be good,' she replied, flashing her dark eyes at him. 'But first, can I get you a drink? I'm going to have a gin and tonic.'

'No, no. Please let me,' he said, before catching the barman's eye. 'A gin and tonic and an orange juice, please.'

'You are not drinking?' she asked, curious.

'I've given up,' Dan said. 'It wasn't good for me.'

Cristina smiled. 'I like a man who knows himself.'

The couple moved, with their drinks, to a quiet corner table and were soon chatting away. Dan told her about his daughter and his recent move to London and search for a job. Cristina then explained how she had left Bucharest for a new life in the UK. She loved her work but the hours in the hospital long and demanding. As she talked, she gave a big yawn.

It was clear that she was completely shattered after her shift the day before.

'I'm sorry, Dan, this has been lovely but think I'd better head back now. Please would you walk me home? I always worry about the nasty strangers you can meet on the towpath at night. And we're both going the same way.'

No answer was necessary. They both buttoned up against the cold night. The moon seemed to be shining even brighter as they left the pub. Cristina grasped his hand in hers, pulling him closer to her as they set off down the towpath chatting together before eventually reaching her block of flats. She stopped outside the main door and pulled Dan towards her – her hands were all over him as she kissed him again and again.

Where next, he wondered? But, after a while, Cristina slowly and reluctantly pulled herself away from his grasp.

'Dan. I really like you. Very much. I would like to see you again but I am now really so very tired. I have to wake up early tomorrow morning because I'm on an early shift again. And so I must say goodnight to you now.' She sounded very upset. 'I will phone you tomorrow. I promise. I so much want to see you again. And very soon.'

She looked up at him longingly, gave him another long, deep kiss, then turned away and walked through the door of her block of flats. And she was gone.

Dan slowly returned to his lonely bed, but again was unable to sleep. He tossed and turned, repeating again and again in his mind his encounter with

Cristina – those dark eyes watching him over the table in the pub. And then, at the end, that kiss, Dan pulling her closer and closer, loving her warmth and her scent.

****

The following morning dragged slowly by for Dan as he sat at his window, checking his email periodically for word about a possible interview and, at the same time, watching to see if Cristina passed by. But there was no sign of her that day. She must have left for the hospital very early indeed. He needed some fresh air, and so later in the day set off for a brisk walk along the canal bank, retracing his steps to and from the Wheatsheaf. Back at the flat he watched the darkening evening draw in like a reluctant snail. Cristina still hadn't called. But he kept his phone close at hand. At 8.00 pm his phone rang. It was Cristina, sounding apologetic.

'Hi Dan. I am so sorry we had to end it so early last night. It was such a shame. I just was so tired and I couldn't stay awake.'

'No problem,' replied Dan encouragingly. 'I do understand.'

'But I'd love to see you again,' replied Cristina, her warm Romanian accent sounded inviting. 'I am free tomorrow evening and have the day off the next day.'

'That sounds good to me,' he replied.

'Meet me at my place at eight?' she suggested. And Dan agreed.

****

The following evening Dan arrived at Cristina's flat and she buzzed him into the building. He knocked on her door and when it opened he gasped. She was wearing the same stunning, low-cut dress she had worn before at the King James on New Year's Eve. Dan was not sure what to say and so it was Cristina who spoke first. She had a shy smile on her face as she invited him into her flat.

'Well? What do you think? Will I do for you?' she asked.

'Oh yes,' he replied, as he threw his arms around her, pulling her very close, kissing her over and over and feeling her warmth. He found himself wanting to take things further. But Cristina had another idea. As she slowly pulled herself away from him she was smiling.

'Let's go and get something to eat first,' she said. 'Do you like Italian food?'

'Yes, I sure do!'

'Well, you are in for a treat! I know just the place for us. My friend, Maria, works there. They have the most amazing Italian food.'

They set off down the towpath to Bella Cucina, which overlooked the canal.

As they neared the restaurant, they could hear the sound of sirens and see the blue flashing lights of police cars and an ambulance on the nearby bridge. They walked slowly towards the restaurant where they joined a group of onlookers, looking concerned and chatting to each other. Dan approached one of the group and asked what was going on.

'Dunno, mate,' he said. 'Looks like someone has ended up in the canal? That does seem to happen here. Favourite spot, you know. It's bound to be drug-related. Not very nice really.'

'Oh no, that sounds awful!' exclaimed Dan who could see that Cristina was looking very disturbed. He put his arm around her to comfort her and found she was shuddering.

'All this is making me think of my work at the hospital,' she said. 'I am dealing with things like this every day.'

Dan and Cristina went inside and were soon sitting in a discrete corner.

Maria came over, smiling at Cristina and holding two menus.

'Hi, Cristina,' she said to her friend, 'it's really good to see you again.'

Cristina stood up and they kissed each other on both cheeks. 'And this is my new friend, Dan,' she said, introducing him as he also stood up. Cristina looked at him quizzically, and Dan realised that she must recognise Matt in his features. The two brothers did not now look identical but they looked very similar.

Cristina paused, and her eyes wandered over the canal and all that seemed to be going on over there.

'By the way,' Cristina said, 'we were wondering what has happened over there by the canal.'

Maria's face darkened. 'Oh, yes, apparently they found something in the canal this afternoon. They've just finished searching the area. They've been there all day.'

'Do you mean they found a body?'

'I'm not sure,' Maria said, but she seemed troubled and distracted. 'Anyway, what can I get you both?'

'I'll have a red wine and Dan will have a coke,

please,' Cristina smiled at Dan.

After a while, they could see through the window as the police cars disappeared into the dark and the ambulance set off carrying a sombre cargo. There was quiet at last and they put the incident to the back of their minds.

'So, Dan, tell me more about yourself.' She put her hand over his on the table. 'I only know a little about you – that you have recently moved to London and are seeking a new job. And that you have a beautiful daughter – Maya, right? But where is Maya's mother? Were you married?'

'Well,' said Dan, 'Maya's mother and I were together for a long time but we never married. We separated recently. She found someone else.'

'Oh no!' exclaimed Cristina but then she paused and smiled. 'Although maybe you will also move on now – possibly with the person who is sitting opposite you now?'

'I'd like that,' replied Dan. 'I haven't met anyone I was really interested in having a relationship with... until I met you.'

'And your daughter,' Cristina asked. 'She is a big part of your life, yes?'

'Oh yes,' Dan said. 'But Maya is eighteen now – almost nineteen. She's at Maynard College in her first year at University of London. She is a big part of my life but she needs me around less than she did before. In fact, I'd like to start building a future of my own now.'

'Maybe it is lucky me, then,' said Cristina, grinning at him.

Cristina looked directly into Dan's eyes and spoke to him in a soft and persuasive voice.

'Now it is my turn to tell you all about me. So I moved to the UK for a new life but… the fact is that I do have a husband back home in Romania.'

Dan was dumbstruck and did not know how to reply to this sudden revelation. He just shook his head.

'No, no, no!' exclaimed Cristina. 'Please don't worry. Our marriage is all but over. Constantin and I married when we were very young. I fell in love with him. I was so young that I couldn't resist him. But eventually I wanted children. And Constantin had different plans about our marriage.' Cristina looked sad. 'And there were other women,' she added.

'Is that why you left him and came over to the UK?' asked Dan.

'Yes, of course.' Cristina nodded her head vigorously.

'And so… when did this all happen?' asked Dan.

'Last year. I was just tired of the heartbreak and I wanted to try and start a life of my own. And I so badly want children.' Cristina paused and added. 'I'd always hoped to meet a man who wanted a family too.' She looked as if she was about to burst into tears. She paused before continuing. 'I came to London because I already had an older brother over here. He works as a translator. He lives not so far from here so that was why I chose this part of London. It makes me feel safer to be near to family.'

Dan realised that the man Matt had seen her with was her brother. Not that it mattered now. He just longed to be holding her in his arms.

'Let's go when we have finished our meal. Dan, I want to take you home with me. I have something special for you.'

Dan wondered what precisely she meant, but had high hopes of what it might be. After paying the bill, the couple set off along the moonlit canal path and soon reached Cristina's building.

Cristina quietly opened the front door and took Dan upstairs to her flat, where she carefully closed the door behind them. She removed her coat and flung her arms around him, holding him very close, kissing him. She pulled him into the dim light of her bedroom. Clothes were ripped off and Dan could now see Cristina in all her dark, naked beauty as she lay down on the bed and pulled him down to her. She was soon crying out again and again, begging for more. When it was all over they fell into a long, deep sleep, curled up on the bed together.

****

But Dan's night was not restful. He found himself startled out of sleep and a worried-looking Cristina staring at him. It was the middle of the night.

'What's wrong?' Dan asked.

'You were having a nightmare, I think,' she said gently. 'Dan, you started groaning and crying out and your arms and legs were thrashing the bedclothes. It woke me up. I was so scared. You were moaning some words… "She is gone. She's under the water. Drowning. Disappearing. Help me, someone. For God's sake please help me." What on earth were you dreaming about?'

Dan was now fully awake and gradually calmed down, muttering to himself as he realised that he had been having his familiar nightmare about the day Sophie died.

'It's OK,' he said. 'I sometimes have nightmares about something that happened last year. I'll explain it another time.' Cristina began stroking his hair to calm him just as if he were a distressed child.

After a while they again fell fast asleep. And Dan was not visited by the nightmare again that night. All was well.

Chapter 21

Spring was definitely in the air. Banks of golden daffodils were bursting into flower in the London parks and gardens. Some weeks had passed and things were looking good for Dan. He had secured a new job at the local firm of estate agents and was bringing in a decent salary. Maya was working through the second half of her first year and had introduced both her mother and father to James – on separate occasions. Dan very much approved of the young man.

But not everyone was feeling so happy. Matt's relationship with Maria was still very much alive but her husband was becoming even more controlling of his wife.

Maria had slipped to see Matt on her way back from her job at Bella Cucina late one night. Dan was fast asleep as Matt let her in through the front door of their flat. They kissed passionately.

'I've missed you so much,' Matt said.

'And I've missed you, too,' she answered. She looked pale and worried.

They then made their way into the lounge with cups of coffee. Matt looked at her and was worried. She was shaking at the prospect of heading to her own home as she sipped her drink. Her husband was likely to kill her if he found out she was here. Matt realised that he had fallen in love with this woman. But he was frightened at the thought of what might happen. He knew that they were both in danger.

'Leave him,' he said. It wasn't the first time he had suggested this to her and so she did not look surprised.

'I don't know what he'll do.'

'You don't know what he'll do if you stay with him. Why don't you come and live with me?'

'But Matt—'

'I'll keep you safe. Don't worry. You can hide with us for a while. You and I can move away. Somewhere that Francesco doesn't know about. Where he can't find you.'

Maria looked at him. She cared very much for Matt. She had never ever cheated on her husband before.

They decided not to tell anyone about their plan. Not even Dan – well, not the whole plan anyway. They couldn't risk Maria's husband finding out what she planned to do. Francesco was due to travel on business one weekend and would leave on the Friday afternoon. And Maria saw her chance to get out. Matt had told Dan that he was going to see Maria later that night but he didn't tell his brother that he intended to bring her back to the flat and away from her husband for good.

Friday arrived and that night the moon was full. Matt and Maria had decided that she would leave her flat after midnight to lessen the chances of anyone who knew her seeing her. Likewise, Matt wanted to make sure nobody who might know Francesco saw him leaving the building suspiciously late, so he left his flat early and walked to the pub alone. Anyone who recognised him would simply see him having an innocent drink on a Friday night. He would sneak into Maria's building just as everything was closing up for the night and they would get out and back to his together without anyone noticing. Francesco would have no idea where to look for her. She would be safe.

Outside the pub, Matt was getting concerned about anyone spotting him entering Maria's building. He gave her a quick call.

'Hello, my love. Can I come over soon? I don't think anyone will see me.'

'Sure, OK then,' replied Maria. 'I'll be at the intercom to buzz you right in. I'm ready.'

Inside Maria and Francesco's flat, Maria was preparing to leave. She had an almost full suitcase open on their bed and another two bags all ready to go.

'Matt,' she said, 'you really are the best thing that has ever happened to me.' Suddenly, she looked anxiously around the room. Scared as if Francesco was there, watching them. 'He won't find us, will he? We must make sure that he does not find out about us. I am afraid that we will be in terrible trouble if he does.'

Matt held her close and felt how frightened she was.

'I promise. I will look after— Oh no!'

Matt was abruptly interrupted by the sound of the main door to the flat opening and a bellowing voice calling Maria's name.

'Oh no, Matt!' hissed Maria. 'We are in real trouble now. That's Francesco. He must have come home early. What can we do?' She was getting hysterical. 'You must get out of here... Matt, he'll kill you.'

Francesco could be heard coming down the corridor and approaching the bedroom. There was no way for Matt or Maria to get out of the flat without passing him. Matt knew they would have to face him. Francesco flung open the door of the bedroom and pushed into the room in a fury. He spotted the suitcase first and then Matt.

'*Bastardo*! *Bastardo*!'

Francesco reached out an arm and flung the open suitcase onto the floor and, with a roar, he lunged at Matt. Matt tried to dodge around him and ended up running across the hall into the kitchen. Francesco followed as Maria watched in horror.

A fight then broke out. Matt, like his brother, was strong and a match for Maria's husband. He managed to manoeuvre himself so that he stood between Francesco and the door, with Maria behind him in the hall. For a second, he thought the two of them could make a run for the front door and get out. Then Francesco picked up a large kitchen knife and threatened Matt. Maria screamed. She could see that Francesco was holding the knife and she prayed that Matt would get away from him safe and sound. She started shouting at her husband, begging him to calm down.

'Maria,' Matt shouted, his eyes fixed on the knife held by the man before him, 'get out of here. Get away from him now before he attacks you.'

Maria glanced at the front door. But she couldn't

leave Matt. She ran to the bathroom, locking the door firmly behind her.

Locked in the bathroom, Maria could hear the fight happening in her kitchen. But finally there was a loud shout from Matt and the sound of a door slamming – followed by a sudden silence. Maria was very worried. She had no idea what had happened and desperately hoped that Matt had escaped from Francesco's clutches. Even though it now sounded quiet, she dared not leave the security of the locked bathroom.

In fact, Maria waited an hour until she heard the sound of someone coming back into the flat. She prayed it was Matt. There was a knock on the bathroom door.

'For God's sake, let me in, Maria!' It was Francesco. Her heart sank. 'I don't know how long you've been planning this but that guy is very dangerous. He's crazy. He chased me out of the flat with that knife and I lost him along the towpath.'

Maria said nothing. That didn't sound quite right. Matt hadn't grabbed the knife when she saw them fighting in the kitchen. It had been Francesco who had picked up the knife.

Maria stayed quiet and let Francesco shout at her. She was terrified. Her husband sounded unhinged, ranting at her. And anyway, where was Matt? He was obviously not there.

A fist suddenly slammed into the other side of the door that made her jump.

'Maria!' Francesco sounded more like his usual self now. 'Open this fucking door. Don't make me break it down to get to you.'

Maria slowly turned the lock on the bathroom

door and looked at her husband. He was covered in blood.

'See for yourself what your man has done to me. He attacked me,' Francesco exclaimed angrily. 'He was fast but I managed to get away.'

Maria did not answer. She was still very shocked at what had happened.

Francesco made his way into the kitchen and poured himself a stiff drink. Maria followed him, spotting drops of blood on the hall carpet by the door to the flat. Whose blood was that?

'You've made a big mistake,' Francesco said, downing the glass of whisky he had poured. 'You're going to make it up to me. And you're never going to do anything like this again.'

He slammed the glass down on the counter and grabbed Maria by her hair, pulling her towards him. Maria whimpered and tried to pull away.

'Where is he?' she cried.

'You are going to make it up to me,' Francesco repeated. He pulled her roughly toward their bedroom.

'Francesco,' she pleaded, 'I don't want to. Please.'

'You are *my* wife.'

Maria had been raped by Francesco before, but this was like never before. He was fuelled by a wild fury and Maria was terrified. As she lay awake afterwards, bruised and sore, she quietly wept as many possibilities passed through her mind. What had really happened that evening. What had happened to Matt? Had he got away from Francesco's raging anger? Was he safe?

As she lay there she remembered her husband

growling, 'I will kill you, Maria, if you do anything like this again.'

When she eventually drifted into an exhausted and fitful sleep, she dreamed that she and Matt had gone down to the sea, and were standing hand-in-hand as they watched the waves roll in, over and over again, one after the other. But then a huge wave appeared and crashed down on top of them. They were overcome by the water.

Matt was swept away from her, down into dark rolling waves.

Chapter 22

Earlier that evening, as Matt had been making his way across the canal to fetch Maria, Dan was waiting for Cristina to arrive at their flat. Matt had told him that he was seeing Maria that night and to expect him home very late, so Dan was looking forward to having the flat to himself with Cristina for a few hours.

He was preparing to start their meal when there was a knock at the door. He was surprised to see it was Cristina.

'You're early,' he said, checking his watch. Anyway it is really good to see you.'

'I'm sorry,' she said. 'I needed to talk to you. Something has happened.'

Dan opened the door and let her inside. They made their way into the kitchen and he offered her a drink, but she didn't want one. She didn't even want to take her coat off.

'What's wrong?' Dan asked. She looked agitated.

'Dan,' Cristina began falteringly, 'we've had such a great time together. I care about you very much…'

'What are you trying to say?' he interrupted, although he guessed he knew the answer. He just didn't know why she was saying it.

'It's Constantin,' she said. 'We've been talking recently. On the phone. He says that he wants to try again. He wants us to have a family.'

'But what about the other women?'

'He's changed. He's really changed,' Cristina exclaimed.

'*We* could have started a family,' Dan said, quickly.

'I care about you, Dan, I do. But we've only been seeing each other for a couple of months,' she said. 'I've known Constantin for a lifetime already. He's still my husband.'

'But I've fallen in love with—'

'I know,' she said, softly. 'And I love you, too. But I also love Constantin. And I have to see if we can make it work. Do you understand?'

Dan was silent for a moment. He realised that there was no point in trying to persuade her to stay. It was over.

'I'll try,' he said.

Cristina smiled and hugged him.

'Do you want to stay for dinner?' he asked, feeling foolish.

'No,' she said. 'Thank you, but no. I think it's best if I go now. I've handed in my notice at the hospital and on the flat. I'm flying home in a month. I think it's best if we leave this here now. It was wonderful being with you, Dan. Thank you.'

She turned around and made her way down the hall to the door. Dan watched her leave. There was nothing else to say. He was alone again.

Alone in the flat, Dan was depressed. He felt dismayed at the abrupt ending of it all. He wished his brother would get home so that they could talk over what had happened. But midnight came and went and there was no sign of Matt. Sitting in front of the TV, Dan suddenly developed an acute, ear-splitting headache. And then a feeling of absolute dread. He had a sudden recollection of the day he'd known his brother was hurt before anyone else could tell his mother.

Without giving it too much thought, Dan straightaway phoned Matt, his hand trembling as he held the phone to his ear. But the phone didn't ring and went straight to voicemail. An hour later he called again. There was still no reply. He felt uneasy. Maybe he shouldn't panic. He wondered if perhaps Matt had switched his phone off in order to spend the evening with Maria uninterrupted. He went to bed, but could not sleep.

Dan was still very worried the next morning. Matt had not come home. He tried phoning him but again there was no reply. He put the phone down, seriously confused.

He went through various possibilities. Had Matt lost his phone? Had he left it behind somewhere? Why wasn't it ringing? Had it run out of battery? Had he been involved in an accident? Was he in hospital?

He looked up the number and called the local hospital. No. There had been nobody by the name of Matt Barnes admitted last night. And no unnamed men in their late thirties or early forties. Should he call the police?

Matt had been going to see Maria that night. Dan knew that. Had they met up? Did she know where his brother was? Dan decided to risk calling Maria. He messaged Cristina. Could she please let him have Maria's number. Matt hadn't come home and he needed to speak to her. Cristina responded immediately with Maria's number and said she hoped Matt turned up soon.

Dan called the number. But she didn't pick up. Ten minutes later Dan tried again. This time she picked up.

'Hello? Maria?' he enquired, 'is that you?'

'Yes, yes,' came the reply.

'It's Dan. Matt's brother. He hasn't come back home. Did you meet last night?'

Maria paused before answering. 'Yes, Matt was here. But he's not here now. He hasn't come back to the flat yet?'

'No he hasn't,' said Dan. 'And his phone is going straight to voicemail. What time did he leave?'

Maria didn't answer but Matt could hear a man's voice in the background. It didn't sound like his brother.

'I'm sorry,' she said, quickly. 'I have to go. I am sure he will be home soon.' The line went dead.

When the conversation had finished Dan sat down at the kitchen table, his head in his hands. Something wasn't right. Something had happened. He knew it. Where was his brother?

****

Evening fell and there was still no sign of Matt. Dan

had tried to call Maria again but she hadn't picked up. He then tried sending text messages but they all went unanswered. Something didn't add up. Dan decided that the time had now come to contact the police. On the Sunday morning he walked to the police station.

He arrived there and told the officer on the desk that his brother was missing. The officer took a few details and then disappeared to fetch a liaison officer. Dan was taken into a private room and interviewed by a police officer who introduced herself as DC Patel.

'It's your brother who you are concerned about?' she said.

'My twin brother,' Dan confirmed. He passed over the desk a photograph of Matt that he had brought with him. DC Patel examined the photo.

'You're quite similar,' she noted. 'Almost identical if it wasn't for the beard. And Matthew Barnes is thirty-nine?'

'Almost forty.'

'When and where did you last see him?'

'Friday evening. At his flat. I gave the address to your colleague. I'm staying with him. I have been for a few months.'

'And where was he going?'

'He was going out for a drink and then he was going to meet a woman he has been seeing.'

'A woman? And her name?'

'Maria. Maria Cimmino. She's... Maria is married. She and Matt were having an affair.' DC Patel raised an eyebrow and indicated that Dan should continue. 'Matt told me that her husband has a reputation for violence. His name is Francesco. Francesco Cimmino. I don't know exactly in which flat they live, but their building is fairly close to where we are.'

'Have you been in touch with Mrs Cimmino?'

'Yes, I had to ask a friend for her number. She told me that Matt had been there but he had left and she didn't know where he was. She sounded… odd. I don't know how to explain it. She hasn't responded to any of my messages since then.'

'We'll get in touch with her,' DC Patel said, noting down the details on a pad. 'No mental health issues? I mean, your brother…'

Dan paused before answering. 'Errr… his little daughter died last year. She was six. She drowned. Things were very difficult but Matt was dealing with it all. But I really don't understand all this. He wouldn't just disappear.'

'OK Mr Barnes, I realise that this is very difficult for you and the family, and for you particularly. But I have a few more questions, if you don't mind?'

'Of course, no problem.'

'This man, Francesco Cimmino,' DC Patel said. 'You say Matthew told you he was violent. Have you ever seen any evidence of that?'

'No,' Dan said, thinking back to the only time he had seen Maria's husband – on New Year's Eve. 'But Matt was serious. He told me that Francesco was violent towards his wife. She wanted to leave him. But she was scared to. DC Patel, I'm honestly worried that something has happened to my brother and it has something to do with this man.'

'We'll be going to speak to the Cimminos,' DC Patel confirmed. 'In the meantime, I suggest you contact any close family or friends to check that Matthew has not been in touch with them. If you find that he has, or if you think of anything else, please do contact us.'

DC Patel stood up and handed Dan a card with contact details over the table. They shook hands and Dan left the police station.

Dan walked quickly down the canal path to their building. He just could not accept the fact that his brother was missing. Maybe he would find that Matt had called someone – their father, Lisa, even his work – and he would feel overwhelming relief. He entered the empty flat and made himself a coffee. He checked his watch and calculated the time difference. It didn't matter. He needed to speak to his father.

'Dad?' Dan said when the line picked up.

'Dan,' his father sounded very distant. 'Hello. Are you OK?'

'Dad, have you heard from Matt recently?'

'Let me see. Last week. Yes, he called me on his way home from work to catch up.'

'No. I mean since Friday afternoon – our time.'

'Sorry. No. Not a thing. Why? What's wrong?'

Dan took a deep breath and said, 'I don't know where he is, Dad. I think he may be missing.'

'What? How— I mean, why?'

'I've contacted the police, Dad. They're investigating.'

'Listen, Dad. I need to speak to Lisa. Just in case Matt has called her recently. Do you have a number for her? I don't know if the one I have is recent.'

'I... I think she's on the same number, Dan. She understandably hasn't been in touch with me since she and your brother decided to separate.'

'I'll try the number I have.'

'Keep me posted.'

'I'll find him, Dad. Love you.'

Dan hung up. He flicked through his contacts until he found the number for Lisa Barnes. And he dialled it.

'Lisa, it's Dan here. Dan Barnes.'

'Dan? Why are you calling? Is Matt OK?'

'You haven't heard from him recently? Matt, I mean…'

'No… of course not. Why would I—? Where is he?'

'The problem is that I don't know. He went out on Friday and we haven't seen him since.'

'Oh my God. Have you—'

'I just got off the phone with Dad. He hasn't heard from him,' Dan answered her before she finished her question. Dan briefly wondered about telling Lisa the whole story. Did she even know Matt was seeing another woman? Maybe Lisa was also seeing someone new. Before he had time to decide Lisa made an announcement.

'I'm getting a flight back home.'

'Lisa, you don't have to—'

'I do, Dan. This isn't what Matt does. Something has happened to him. We might have split up but he's my husband still. I'll call you when I figure out how to get to London. Keep me posted.'

Dan felt relieved that he had at last made contact with Lisa. He had actually missed her – her long blonde hair and the twinkle in those blue eyes. But the terrible death of her daughter Sophie had changed everything between him and his sister-in-law.

Chapter 23

On Monday morning there was still no word from Matt. Dan called Matt's employer's office from his desk at the estate agents and had an awkward conversation with the receptionist. Was his brother there? No, Matt hadn't come in yet, which was odd as it was now 9.45. Was he running late? Dan then explained the situation to the woman and she assured him that she would tell Matt's line manager and pass on Dan's details. And of course they would cooperate with the police. Dan put the phone down. Job done.

After a while his mobile rang. It was the police asking him to go to the police station for an update. Dan stood up and shouted to his boss who was sifting through listings by the printer.

'Jeremy, that was the police. I've got to go.'

'Sure thing, Dan. Hope they've got good news for you.' Jeremy gave him a nod and a thumbs-up.

As Dan made his way to the station his mind raced. Had they found Matt? Was he OK? Had they discovered a body? He felt sick at the idea. He arrived at the police station and was shown into the private room where DC Patel and another officer were waiting for him. He was feeling very nervous as he sat down.

'Good morning, Mr Barnes, and thanks for coming in again,' she said. 'I know things are very difficult for you at the moment, but we need to update you. An officer went and spoke with Mr and Mrs Cimmino on Sunday evening. Neither of them denied that Matthew was at their home on Friday but they both say that he left. In fact, Mr Cimmino said that Matthew tried to attack him with a knife and he threw him out. His wife confirms his account.'

'What?' Dan felt incredulous. 'That doesn't make any sense. Matt would never threaten anyone with anything. Are you sure you spoke to Maria?'

'We did, Mr Barnes. But there is another angle. There's a lot of CCTV at the establishments in that area and we hit something from the first footage we acquired from the Bella Cucina restaurant. Around midnight, you can see two men – one clearly in pursuit of the other – running past. The footage is grainy so it's not clear whether either of these men is Matthew.'

'That must have been Matt,' Dan said, feeling suddenly desperate. 'That Francesco must have chased him. Maria has to be lying. He beats her, you know. She's terrified of him. That's why she's lying. He's done something to my brother.'

'Please, Mr Barnes,' DC Patel said quietly. 'I know how hard this must be for you. We'd like to place some posters with a picture and some information about Matthew around the canal. We're hoping we can get some leads on your brother's whereabouts or anyone who might have seen anything. We will be approaching the news media, too.'

'What about the canal? Are you going to look in the canal?' Dan hardly dared ask.

'Bella Cucina is some distance from where Matthew was last seen and we're not sure whether that was him on the footage. We'd like to narrow down where we search, if possible.'

'Give me the posters,' Dan said, quickly. 'I'll put them up today. Right now.'

'That would be most helpful,' DC Patel said.

****

Dan was stapling posters of his brother's smiling face to the telephone poles that ran up and down the canal when he got a call from Lisa.

'I'm flying back tomorrow. I should be with you by Thursday early evening. Is there any news? Have you heard from him?'

'No, I'm sorry, Lisa. There's nothing from Matt. The police have checked CCTV of a local restaurant though and they might have caught Matt. He was running away from someone.'

'What? No! He's been hurt, hasn't he?'

'I really don't know, Lisa. I just don't know.' Dan felt close to tears. He could hear Lisa was crying on the other end of the phone, too.

'Look. I'm on my way,' she said, taking a deep breath. 'I'll call you when I land.' She hung up.

Dan finished stapling the poster and noticed that he was just steps away from Bella Cucina. The door to the restaurant opened and a fragile-looking Maria stepped outside, pulling her coat around her. She glanced up and saw Dan.

'Maria,' he called, instinctively. 'Please…'

'I can't,' she said, trying to walk quickly past him.

'Please, Maria,' Dan sped up to keep pace with her. 'My brother. Did your husband do something to Matt? Please, Maria. Where is he?'

'I can't, Dan,' she said. 'Please leave me alone. If he sees me talking to you…'

'You lied for him, didn't you?' Dan said. He had been right.

'Please, Dan, I can't do this. Please leave me alone.' Maria was crying now and she broke into a run. Dan didn't want to chase the poor woman down the street. What else could he do? He just had to hope that she would find the courage to tell the police the truth.

Another day with no Matt passed and Dan met Lisa at the Tube station. She looked just as he remembered her but she had an air of tiredness about her now. He thought back to everything she had been through in the last year. It was just over twelve months since she lost her only daughter and then just eight months since her marriage disintegrated. And now her husband was missing.

'Where are you staying?' Dan asked.

'I actually hadn't thought that far ahead,' she admitted. 'Is there a hotel around here?'

'Stay at the flat,' Dan didn't even hesitate. 'You can take my bed. I'll hit the sofa.' He knew neither of them could possibly sleep in Matt's bed.

'I suppose that would be less expensive,' Lisa said. 'Thanks. I forgot to ask over the phone. But why are you living here? Where's Amy and Maya?'

Dan took a deep breath and said, 'Yes. I'll update you on the way back to the flat.

As they walked, Dan told his sister-in-law about how he had found himself living with his brother again. It turned out that Lisa knew through her sporadic contact with Matt that the brothers had reconciled but Matt had kept the details about Dan and Amy's relationship and the fire from her.

Back at the flat, Dan showed Lisa to his room and gave her some fresh linen for the bed. She began to unpack a few belongings whilst he made his way into the lounge. Dan flicked on the television, hoping to catch the local news. The newsreader was halfway through a story about a new train line which was being constructed and was horribly delayed. The next story was the one Dan was interested in.

'Police are appealing for eyewitnesses in the case of a man missing from Camden. Matthew Barnes was last seen leaving a building close to Whitmore Road around midnight on Friday 18th February.' The photograph of the smiling Matt appeared on the screen. 'Anyone who recalls sighting Matthew Barnes after that time is asked to contact the police with details.'

Dan felt Lisa come into the room behind him.

'Want a coffee?' he said, flicking the television set off again.

They sat down at the kitchen table. Dan needed to tell Lisa the whole story. He did so, as gently as he could. Lisa looked momentarily hurt when he told her about Matt and Maria. She clearly hadn't moved on as much as he had.

'So, he was really serious about this woman?' she asked.

'Kind of,' Dan said. 'They hadn't been seeing each other long but it was risky because of her situation with her husband. He'd asked her to leave her husband but mainly because he was abusive.'

'And this man – Francesco – he told the police that Matt was there but that Matt had threatened him with a knife and then left? And she says that's true?'

'That's where we are.'

'She's lying, isn't she? Have you spoken to her?'

'I tried. She won't speak to me. She's scared.'

'Maybe I could speak to her?'

'I don't think that would help. We need to wait and see if anyone saw Matt when he left the flat and where he went.'

'Something has happened to him, I know it.' Lisa's eyes filled with tears.

'I'm so sorry, Lisa,' Dan said. 'I'm so sorry about what happened with you and Matt and I'm so, so sorry about what happened to Sophie. I know you blame me. And I understand.'

'I did blame you,' Lisa said, firmly. 'I honestly hated you. But Matt found it in his heart to forgive or move on somehow. He was heartbroken about Sophie but he found it in himself to release you from the blame. He loves you. And so I'm trying, too.'

'I don't know what to say,' Dan said, sadly. 'I messed up so much. And your marriage...'

'What happened between Matt and me had been a long time in the making,' Lisa said. 'We struggled to have Sophie. We both wanted more children – at least I thought we both did. We were looking at options when we lost her. And Matt just seemed to lose the will to try anymore. Something changed when she died. Every time I mentioned IVF or anything like that – he would shut down. I felt him drifting away from me. From the life I thought we'd have. And I couldn't stay.' Lisa wiped her eyes. 'I just pray that we find him. I can't imagine how I'm going to cope if he's...' She tailed off, unable to say the words that they were both thinking.

Dan nodded. The two sat in silence and drank their coffees. Eventually, nothing left to do, they retired to their beds and hoped for news in the morning.

Chapter 24

The next day, Dan was at work in the estate agents. Jeremy had relieved him of doing any property viewings so that he could answer his phone immediately if there was any news. He was on desk duty but he couldn't concentrate on anything. His phone rang and he picked it up on the first ring.

'Yes, Dan Barnes.'

'Mr Barnes, it's DC Patel. We've had a development.'

'What? Have you found Matt?'

'I'm afraid not but we have had a witness come forward following the news story. The witness is an individual of no-fixed-abode who is known to local authorities. He was at the shelter when he saw the news story last night. But he sometimes finds himself sleeping in doorways along the canal. He was there that night. He witnessed someone who fits the description of your brother struggling with a larger man on the edge of the canal by Haggerston Wharf. He reported that he saw the larger man was brandishing a knife. Fearing for his own safety, the witness didn't stay to see the outcome of this altercation. But he has given us a place to search for Matthew.'

'Thank you.' Dan couldn't think of anything else to say. They were going to start looking for his brother in the canal and that meant he was dead.

'We'll keep you posted,' DC Patel said.

Dan hung up. At this point Dan shuddered and had gone pale. He still could not get his mind around what had exactly happened on that evening. And as for dredging the canal, the whole idea of it made him feel sick.

His worst nightmare had been realised.

****

The following day Dan and Lisa sat in the kitchen. The Marine Police Unit had moved in, setting up cabins on the canalside a little way down the road. The search for a body was well under way. Dan had called in sick to work. Jeremy told him he could take all the time he needed.

Dan's phone rang. He answered. It was DC Patel again.

'Mr Barnes,' she said, 'we've been contacted by Maria Cimmino and she has recanted her original statement.'

'Wait a second,' Dan said, 'my brother's wife is here with me. Let me put you on speaker phone. Go ahead.' Lisa leaned close to hear what the officer had to say.

'Mrs Cimmino is currently under police protection. She has recanted her original statement and given us a very different picture of what happened that night. We are sending a unit to Francesco Cimmino's office where he is thought to be currently. If the unit working by the canal find a body, we will be arresting Cimmino on suspicion of murder.'

Dan watched as Lisa closed her eyes and lowered her head in despair. He knew then that his brother was dead. His twin. Matt. Dan cleared his throat, trying to find the words.

'I... thank you for the information, DC Patel.'

After Dan hung up he stared at Lisa. She looked broken. Her shoulders were shaking with wracking sobs. He hesitantly put his arms around her. She leaned sideways into him, letting him take her weight as she cried.

****

They found a body later that day. DC Patel called Dan to inform him of that and the fact that Francesco Cimmino was under arrest for his brother's murder. The police needed a formal identification of the body, though. Dan quietly thought that all they needed to do was see that the man they had found looked just like him but he knew that procedure had to be followed. He told Lisa he would make the identification and save her that pain.

Later in the day Dan was escorted to the local morgue to see the body they had found in the canal. Dan suddenly found himself transported to that dreadful day in the hospital when he had formally identified the tiny body of Matt's beloved daughter. He was accompanied by a man in a white coat to a cold and clinical room with a strongly antiseptic smell. A trolley was rolled in. There was the shape of a body on the top of the trolley which was completely covered by a white sheet.

'Are you sure you are ready?' asked the man in the white coat.

'Yes, I think so,' replied Dan. 'Just carry on. I think I will be OK.'

The top of the cloth was then pulled back to reveal a cold white face. Dan gasped and looked away. It was his own face. It was his brother's face. Matt was gone.

'Yes,' said Dan in a weak voice, 'this is my brother, Matthew James Barnes.' He paused for a while, taking it all in.

The man in the white coat escorted him out of the room. Dan was distraught. When he got back to the flat Lisa was half-heartedly making some food for their dinner. She looked up at him and he just nodded. Without a word, he made his way into the lounge where he dialled his father's number. Ollie had told Dan to call at whatever time – day or night.

Dan could almost hear his father's heart break over the phone. Poor Ollie had endured so much loss. His beautiful granddaughter, his beloved wife and now his son – all of them taken way before their time. It was everything Dan could do not to jump on a plane and rush to hug his father.

Just after he said goodbye to his father, his phone rang. It was a number he didn't recognise.

'Dan?'

'Yes, who is this?'

'It's Maria. Maria Cimmino.' Dan's breath caught in his throat.

'Maria,' he said. 'What... I mean... do you know what happened today?'

'I do know,' she said. 'I know they found Matt. I wanted to call you – I still had your number from that day you called me to ask about him. Francesco… he had raped me the night before – the night that he found Matt and I together. And he hit me. I was so scared that day. I didn't know what had happened to Matt when he left the flat. And when you said that he was missing, I knew what Francesco had done. I was just so scared.'

'I understand,' Dan said.

'But when I saw the news and the police searching the canal,' Maria continued, 'I knew I had to break free from him. I couldn't let him get away with murdering Matt. I'm so sorry, Dan. If it wasn't for me, Matt would still be here. I'll never forgive myself.'

'It's OK, Maria,' Dan replied. 'It wasn't your fault. Are you safe now?'

'I am. Francesco is in custody. The police have helped me find a place to stay whilst I figure out where to go. I'm leaving London. But, Dan, I've also said that I will testify if I have to. I won't let Francesco get away with this. The police say that my testimony might be what settles the case against him. Even with no physical evidence they say that between me and the CCTV they can put him in prison.'

'That's good, Maria. You are a brave woman.'

'Please forgive me, Dan,' she said, sadly. 'I very much loved your brother and he wanted to help me.'

Dan repeated the conversation for Lisa as they both picked at the pasta she had made.

'Do you think we'll be able to have a funeral soon? For Matt?' she asked.

'I don't know,' Dan said. 'I guess we need to wait until they've carried out an autopsy and everything. I'll organise it all, though. You don't need to worry.'

'No,' Lisa said, firmly. 'I want to help you.'

They ate in silence. Both wondering how anything would ever be the same again.

Chapter 25

Weeks passed. Lisa and Dan felt like they were in some sort of limbo. Francesco Cimmino had been charged with Matt's murder. The police had given them no more news than that. There would be no further movement until the case came to trial. Matt's body remained in the police morgue whilst the police built their case against Cimmino.

Dan went back to work. He was grateful that his boss had been so understanding but he needed a distraction from everything. Lisa spent some time with Maya and kept things at the flat going. Dan had told her she could stay as long as she wanted and she felt that she simply couldn't go anywhere or continue with her life before the trial took place. They ate together every day and went for weekend walks – taking the Tube to places far away from the canal where they had found Matt. Dan had quietly held Lisa as she mourned Matt and remembered her daughter's death as she cried herself into a fitful sleep. She woke up in his arms the next morning and made him a cup of tea. They were like a sad parody of a married couple. Dan quietly thought it ironic that Lisa and Matt had been driven apart by grief for Sophie but that he and Lisa seemed bound together by their grief for Matt. Neither of them spoke about the future. They were trapped in the present together, for now.

It was June before they heard any news on the murder trial. Francesco Cimmino had clearly been advised by his counsel that he stood little chance of convincing a jury that he didn't kill Matt Barnes after such damning testimony from his wife. His best bet was to take a plea deal and this he had done. He pleaded guilty to the murder. Dan was advised that he could hold a funeral for his brother.

****

The day of Matt's funeral was a grey day, the sun hidden by dark clouds looming over north London. Ollie had arrived days before, making the long journey back from Australia alone. He looked pale and drawn and had gripped Dan to him tightly when he met him at the airport. Ollie had taken a room at a hotel. Nobody wanted to sleep in Matt's room and Lisa was still staying at the flat with Dan on the sofa as he had been for weeks. The three of them sat in the car that followed the hearse carrying Matt's body into the crematorium.

As Dan clambered out of the car and turned back to help his father out, he saw that Maya was already here. By her side was James. He watched as Maya went straight over to Lisa and gave her a big hug. She then came over and did the same to him.

'I'm so sorry, Dad,' she whispered in his ear. Then she gently took her grandfather's arm and led him inside.

'We did OK with Maya, didn't we?' a voice next to him said. He turned and saw it was Amy. 'Hi,' she said, smiling kindly. 'I'm so sorry about Matt, Dan. I can hardly believe it. Are you all right?'

Dan shrugged and they embraced.

'I'm OK,' he said. 'And yes, Maya is great. We did that bit right.' They smiled at each other with affection.

'Hi Amy.' Lisa came around the side of the car and hugged Amy. The two women headed into the crematorium as Dan watched the coffin bearers take the white coffin holding his twin brother out of the car and load it onto their shoulders. As they followed the procession, a song that Matt had loved played. It was time to say goodbye to his brother.

Inside, Dan sat between his daughter and Lisa. Maya was looking nervous as she passed a sheet of paper to her father. It had her writing on it.

'This is it, Dad. It's all finished now,' she whispered.

Maya had offered to help Dan with the eulogy he would be giving as part of the service. She had written a poem for her uncle.

'Thanks so much, Maya,' he said as he read the final version. 'This is beautifully written and so positive. You are so thoughtful. Hey, why don't you read this?'

'Oh no, Dad. I couldn't. I wrote it for you to read…'

'Please, Maya. It would mean so much to hear you

read it for your uncle.' Maya smiled and nodded.

The chapel was now beginning to fill up with family, friends and Matt's work colleagues. When everyone was seated there was a sudden hushed silence. Dan turned as the coffin bearers carried his brother down the middle of the congregation. On the back row, he caught sight of a dark-haired woman. She had cut her hair shorter but was still beautiful. He smiled at Maria as he caught her eye and she smiled back, her eyes full of tears.

There then followed the eulogy. Dan and Maya walked purposefully up to the lectern, both clutching their papers.

'Matt and I are twins,' Dan began. 'I don't know that you can get a closer sibling relationship than that. We were close even as kids. I remember so well those walks in the woods, and fishing with Dad and then back to the cottage for scrumptious cakes made by my mum, Maggie. Bless her. Those are days that are imprinted in my memory. They feel just like yesterday. Matt was always the more lively and definitely the naughtiest of us two. In fact he once tripped me up and made me fall into the river on a fishing trip. Dad had to rescue me, getting completely soaked in the process.'

Ollie, seated on the front row, laughed through his tears at the memory. Dan grinned at his father.

'Because we were twins and looked so similar we were intentionally put into separate parallel classes. But we sometimes secretly swapped places. Matt was much better at maths than me and often helped or did my homework. But I was better than him at English.

'Matt grew up to be an amazing man and an amazing father. The loss of his daughter, Sophie, was always something that hung heavy on him but he nevertheless managed to forgive and try and find some hope for the future. He was a good friend. If he cared about you, he would do anything he could to protect you.' Dan searched for and found Maria's eyes at the back of the room. She nodded.

'Matt and I have always had a connection. We have always somehow known when the other one was hurt or in trouble. I remember the first time we realised it. He had been the subject of a bad tackle on the rugby field. I was at home and had a sudden nasty headache. I told my mum immediately that it was because Matt was hurt. She doubted me until the school called her to say that he had passed out and an ambulance had been called.'

Dan paused. Memories of Matt on that afternoon came flooding back to him. Dan pulled himself together, coughed and continued:

'And there was a more recent time. When I was in trouble. I was in a very dark place. And things weren't looking good for me. Matt and I – well, we hadn't spoken for a while – but he knew. Somehow he knew. And, well, that night I think he saved my life.'

Dan paused and looked across at his daughter. He had never told Maya about the night he'd been driven to the edge. She looked worried but then she smiled and nodded at him.

'Matt was taken away far too soon from us by violence. I don't want us to think of the man who took my brother away today. I want to think of Matt and everything he was.'

Dan turned to Maya who had been patiently listening and waiting to read out her poem.

'My daughter, and Matt's niece, Maya, has written a poem for her uncle. Maya, please come here.'

Dan stood aside and pulled out a handkerchief to wipe his eyes. Maya looked around the chapel, adjusted the microphone, coughed nervously and raised her sheet of paper to read. She introduced the poem in a voice which gained confidence as she spoke.

'Dad suggested that I write a poem which turns grief into love. Because it sums up what my uncle was like as a person. It is entitled "Matt's journey".'

Maya looked up at the congregation and then again at Dan, who gave her a thumbs up. He was so proud of her. She cleared her throat and started reading.

'Matt's journey.

Do not think of Matt as gone away,

Lost forever and forever after,

His journey is just another day,

In a new life of love and laughter.

Our Matt has now left behind him

All the sorrows and all the tears,

For now he's in a joyful world,

Where there are no days, nor weeks nor years.

He is living now in the hearts of those he knew,

And sure that nothing would ever be forgotten.

He now has a new life which is forever true.'

The congregation murmured approval as Maya stepped down. She and Dan moved towards their seats again. As Dan sat down, he felt a hand slide into his. Looking down, he saw that it was Lisa's. She was staring straight ahead at the coffin. It was time to finally say goodbye to Matt.

In the background the song 'Always look on the bright side of life' played as Matt's coffin moved towards the opening curtains at the top of the crematorium. Dan smiled to himself. Matt always had a great sense of humour and would have wanted people to smile. Lisa glanced at him and smiled with tears in her eyes, squeezing his hand tightly.

The coffin slowly disappeared beyond the curtains and then closed, taking Matt away from the living world and onto the next. As the congregation filed out, another of Matt's favourite songs 'You'll never walk alone' was played.

The sun had now burst through the dark clouds as they stepped out. Lisa was still holding Dan's hand.

Chapter 26

Cimmino's guilty plea meant that there was no need for a trial, and that meant that there was no need for Maria to testify in court. There was, however, his sentencing. Dan and Lisa both wanted to be there. It had been some weeks since Matt's funeral and the two of them were still living at the flat together. Dan was sleeping on the sofa and Lisa was in his old bed. Matt's room remained empty.

On the day of the sentencing, the two of them made their way by Tube to the courts. They were far too early and had to sit and watch the comings and goings of the court while they waited to be summoned. Finally, they were called. As they sat together in the gallery, Dan felt Lisa slide her hand into his.

Francesco Cimmino was a big man and he shuffled into the court room, bound by hand and leg cuffs and flanked by two prison guards. As he reached the steps to the dock he looked up and stared straight at Dan, who stared back at him. Angry.

The judge cleared his throat and began his sentencing remarks, telling the court that the defence had asked him to bear in mind that this was a crime of passion. Cimmino was sentenced to eighteen years. He would see freedom again but he would be an old man by then. Justice had been done.

After Cimmino was taken back down and the court moved on, Dan and Lisa stepped out onto the court steps into the sunshine.

'What now?' Dan asked.

'I guess it's over,' she said, thoughtfully. 'We could move on now. If we wanted to…'

Dan looked at her. She looked so beautiful in the sunshine. He realised that he cared deeply for her.

Lisa looked back at him then turned and raised one hand to his cheek.

'You always looked so alike,' she whispered. 'And yet, so different.'

'Matt was always the better man.'

'Dan, you *are* a good man.'

'I don't think I want to move on now,' he said, softly. 'I'm not sure I can.'

'What do you mean?' she asked.

'Move on. From this moment,' Dan could hardly believe he had voiced what was pounding in his heart. There was a long pause as he waited for her response.

'Maybe we should move on together?' she said quietly. She slid her hand into his and smiled. They walked hand-in-hand down the steps and back to the flat. Things were looking up for Dan.

Two years later

It was a sunny May afternoon and Birch Cottage had been restored by Ollie to its former glory. It was now home to Ollie who had returned to the UK to live out his years closer to his family. Dan drove up the familiar driveway with Lisa at his side. Ollie was already at the door as they pulled up the drive to the cottage.

'Where is my granddaughter?' he asked, smiling.

'In the back, of course,' replied Dan.

'She's sleeping,' said Lisa, putting her finger to her lips.

Ollie stared at the sleeping baby in the back seat of the car.

'Ah, little Rose,' he cooed. 'She is so precious.'

'Are they here?' Maya bounded out from the cottage. Now a graceful twenty-two year old, she had completed her degree and was training to become a teacher. James followed her out of the house. He was a trainee in a law firm and the two of them had moved into a flat in north London after their engagement six months ago.

Lisa was carefully extracting the sleeping Rose from the car as Dan hugged his daughter and gave James a strong handshake.

'Let's see it, then,' Lisa said to Maya.

Maya proudly held out her left hand where there sparkled a beautiful diamond ring.

'It's lovely, my love,' Dan said, hugging her again. He turned to James and smiled. 'And you are a lucky man, you know.'

'Oh, I know, Mr Barnes, I am really lucky.' said James.

'Please, please do call me Dan now,' insisted Dan.

They all headed inside where Maya had prepared pots of tea for everyone to sit down and enjoy the newly laid-out garden.

The London flat had passed to Lisa as she was still Matt's wife when he died. They decided to sell it and, with Dan's salary they acquired a mortgage on a terraced house not far from where Maya and James were renting in north London. It meant Dan could see his daughter regularly.

Lisa and Dan were now both in their forties. It had been a great shock but a good one when Lisa discovered that she was pregnant. Dan proposed and Lisa gladly accepted. The wedding had been low key. They didn't need a big party. Baby Rose had eventually arrived and sealed their future.

Maya was besotted with her baby sister. Lisa fell right back into motherhood although she often joked about being the oldest mother on the maternity ward. Dan was a father to two now. He still thought about his brother each and every day. And he had not touched a drop of drink since the night Birch Cottage went up in flames.

Amy and Adam were still living in Milchester. Amy and Dan's need to communicate had lessened as Maya became a proper adult. Amy had messaged him when Rose was born and when Maya had told them she was engaged. Dan wished her every happiness in her new life.

As the family chatted over tea and cake and passed baby Rose around the table, Dan's eyes met Lisa's. She smiled at him. They were very happy despite all the bad times they had experienced.

And so the party continued until early evening when people started to grow tired and head to bed. As the sun started to dip down over the distant silhouette of Woodbury Hill, all was quiet. Rose had been put to bed and Dan and Lisa sat in the garden with the rest of the family to watch the sunset. It was spectacular. The whole sky was exploding into a majestic display of crimson and gold.

There was then a miracle of pure magic. A flock of birds appeared out of nowhere, flying in wide circles over the nearby trees and the cottage, calling and warbling, transfixing the family with their birdsong. Round and round they flew, rising and falling in waves again and again, and sending, in their song, a message of goodwill to the spectators.

And so it was. An end and a beginning.

About the Author

Michael Fardon has always had a passion for writing. It first started at The King's School, Worcester where he won first prize for a school history competition. After leaving school he moved on to London University where he greatly enjoyed studying English Literature and began writing his own poetry and stories.

At the successful end of his studies, Michael changed direction, got married and working in London for an international bank – a move which he needed to make to support a growing family.

In later years, Michael established an educational publishing company, Osborne Books, which is still helping students with their exams today.

He is very much a family man with five children and four grandchildren.

Acknowledgements

This is a big thank you to all those who have helped me with writing *Through Dark Waters*. These individuals include Catrin Meredith who has proofread the whole text and to Jo Gooderham who has given excellent advice on content. Thanks must also go to the support and advice of all our grown-up children, Cathy, Rob, Sarah, Tom and Ben.

Last, but not least, Caroline Goldsmith has brilliantly managed and edited the whole book which you now have in front of you.